PET RESCUE PANTHER

BODYGUARD SHIFTERS #2

ZOE CHANT

Pet Rescue Panther

Author's Note

This book stands alone and contains a complete HEA romance. However, if you'd like to read the other books in the series, here's the complete series in order:

You may also enjoy Bodyguard Shifters Collection 1, collecting books 1-4.

CHAPTER 1

Oh hell, not again, was Ben Keegan's first thought when he pulled into his condo's parking lot to find a long black limo parked in his spot.

Dad was here for a visit.

Yay.

It'd been a long goddamn night. Every day as a cop was a long goddamn day, and night shifts were the worst—and he didn't want to deal with this shit at home too. Nevertheless, here it was, in the form of a massive, armored black limo, parked in *his* space.

With a certain amount of vindictive glee, Ben parked his truck behind the limo. He ignored the glare from his dad's driver, a six-and-a-half-foot slab of muscle with a buzz cut and a visible gun bulge under his jacket, leaning on the door of the limo. "Subtle" was not in Darius Keegan's vocabulary.

Neither was "calling ahead."

"You know you're parked in a resident space, right?" Ben asked mildly as he got out of his car. Too bad he was a plain-clothes detective; a patrol car and uniform would've come in

1

handy right about now. "Visitor parking's around at the front."

Muscles ignored him.

"Hey," Ben said, letting a hint of threat slip into his calm voice. "I'm talking to you. Got a permit for that gun, buddy?"

Muscles turned to look down at him. He was *huge*. Ben couldn't help wondering where his dad had scraped this guy up from, and what, if anything, he shifted into. The spiky top of what looked like a jail tattoo was visible under the edge of his collar on his bull-thick neck, and he wore a nose ring for that extra air of class.

Ben was just a shade over six feet tall, he wasn't that powerfully built, and he was used to people underestimating how strong he really was. From Muscles' look of disdain, that was happening here.

"Look, *buddy*," Muscles said at last, in a voice that was surprisingly soft for someone so huge. "I know you're the boss's kid, so I won't rough you up too bad. But he ain't here. And just between you, me, and the wall, having a cop around is bad for business. I've been itching to put a fist in that pretty-boy face of yours."

"Go ahead, give me a reason to arrest you. Assaulting an officer is a pretty good one."

"Yeah, let's see you arrest me while you're picking up your teeth off the ground," Muscles growled, and swung a punch with a massive fist that was probably capable of knocking out a full-grown cow.

He looked really startled when Ben wasn't where he had been a split second ago.

Ben sidestepped casually, hooked his foot behind Muscles' ankle, and yanked. As he did so, he dodged Muscles' backswing, caught the other man's arm, and used Muscles' own momentum to swing him around and slam him into the side of the limo, doubling him up over the hood as Ben twisted his arm behind him.

"I *said* you're under arrest."

"Gonna fuckin' knock your teeth out," Muscles growled.

"Maddox."

The quiet voice came from the building's side entrance. Ben couldn't help noticing that his dad was using the exact same tone of mild disapproval, with an underlying hint of threat, that Ben had used on Muscles earlier.

Except when Darius Keegan did that, it got results in a way Ben had never quite managed to get for himself. Muscles—Maddox—instantly went still and quit trying to free himself as Darius strolled out into the sunlight.

Ben had taken after his mother's slighter build. Although there was still a family resemblance, especially in their sharp, defined facial features, Darius was huge, bigger than Maddox. Every crease in his charcoal-gray suit was crisp. Twin wings of white hair swooped from his temples, but otherwise he showed little sign of age—unsurprising, since he hadn't aged much in the last two hundred years.

He looked at Ben with eyes the color of polished steel.

"Son, what have I told you about beating up the help?"

"Probably similar to what you've told me about arresting the help, which is the other thing I'm gonna be doing in a minute." Ben snapped handcuffs on a now-unresisting Maddox. "You have the right to remain silent—"

Darius ticked his tongue against the back of his teeth. "I'd rather you didn't. It's such a legal hassle getting them out."

"Yeah, well, teach them not to swing punches at cops, then. Anything you do or say can be held against you in a court of law—"

"But that's what I hire them for." A slight smile tugged at the corner of his father's mouth.

Damn it. Having a dragon mobster for a father would've

been so much less complicated if he could have just earnestly hated the guy. "You have the right to an attorney," he continued doggedly.

"When you're done playing your charade of enforcing human law," his father said, "I'll be upstairs having a drink. We need to talk about your sister."

Ben's head swiveled to follow Darius as he turned to walk away. "Wait, what?"

~

A few minutes later, Ben was pouring drinks for both of them in the living room of his condo. A recently un-arrested Maddox was downstairs moving the limo to a legal parking space. Ben decided to consider that a small victory, which were few and far between when dealing with his dad.

Right now Darius was strolling around the condo, investigating the art objects displayed on shelves and hanging on the walls. Ben had brought them back from the various parts of the world he'd visited through the years. Most were weapons of some kind, or otherwise related to battle.

"This is not a particularly valuable hoard, son, but it is an intriguing one," Darius remarked, tapping the blade of a Revolutionary War-era Hessian cavalry sword. "I like it."

"It's not a hoard," Ben said, capping the bottle of brandy—his dad's preferred drink. He'd already gotten a beer for himself. "*You* have a hoard. I have an art collection."

"Call it what you like. I know a hoard when I see one." Darius's eye fell on one of the few truly sentimental touches in the room, a framed photo of Derek and Gaby's wedding. Gaby was visibly pregnant, and Ben's cabin could be glimpsed in the background.

4

Darius picked it up. "Bringing others to your lair? I taught you better, son."

Ben snatched the photo away. "It's not a lair. It's a cabin. And it's none of your damn business. I'm not a dragon, Dad."

"Which is actually why I'm here, Benedict. For a change, my failure to breed a true heir is an advantage."

Darius's words were nearly drowned out by the low growl of the panther in Ben's chest. Ben soothed his animal with an effort. He'd had a lifetime to get used to the way his father felt about him. The most annoying thing about it was that Darius always framed it as a failure in *himself* as much as in Ben. The air of disappointment that permeated every conversation with his father was primarily self-directed. Which paradoxically made it feel even more like his fault as if Darius had openly blamed Ben for it.

Well, that's what you get for being such a self-absorbed asshole that you view your children as extensions of yourself, he thought in Darius's direction.

"How is it an advantage?" Ben asked, as his animal calmed inside him, though it remained on edge, as it always was around his father.

"Because you can do things I cannot." Darius tapped his fingertips on the edge of a Maasai shield. Ben couldn't help imagining phantom dragon's claws clattering thoughtfully on the wood. "This is a dragon matter. I am honor-bound not to interfere. You, on the other hand ..."

Ben snorted. He leaned a hip against the arm of his couch and took a sip of his beer. Darius hadn't touched his drink— probably considered bourbon too cheap for his palate. "Yeah, we all know that's how you feel about lesser shifters, even your own kid. We're beneath your notice unless you find a use for us." He sighed and took another drink, rolled the beer around on his tongue, tried to let it go. "You said earlier that this has to do with my sister. With Melody."

5

With the dragon daughter you've always preferred to your panther-shifter son.

Darius hesitated for a moment before he said. "It's actually to do with a friend of hers. A human friend." Disdain curled around his words. "This friend went and got herself dragon-marked."

There was a brief silence as Ben looked flatly at his father, waiting for an explanation that never came. Finally he said, "And?"

Darius heaved a sigh. "You don't know what that means, do you."

"I was raised by Mom. I know nothing about dragon culture."

"It means she has a dragon assassin after her. They can't be stopped, will stop at nothing, until they kill their target."

"Wait, what? This target—you said she's a human, right?" He forced himself to think about it objectively, engaging his inner cop, not thinking about the human who probably didn't even know about dragons, who would never understand the danger bearing down on her until it was too late ... "Sending a dragon to kill a human is like using a bazooka to kill a fly. It's total overkill. What did she *do*?"

"I don't know," Darius said.

He's lying, Ben's panther said immediately.

Cats were highly alert to nuance, and Ben's panther could pick up on minute changes in people's breathing, heart rate, even the smell of their skin. It wasn't foolproof, but he figured his panther was about as good as your average lie detector. Better, maybe, around people he knew well.

But admitting it would give away one of the few advantages he had in dealing with dragons, not to mention that he knew full well his dad, when caught in a lie, merely doubled down on it.

"So this dragon is after this woman for no reason at all," he said dryly.

"It's no concern of mine," Darius said. Another lie. "One thing I know for certain: when the dragon assassin catches up with her, she has no chance at all. Whether you want to help her or not is up to you."

"And here you are, not interfering."

Darius lifted a shoulder in the tiniest of shrugs. "Merely bringing a situation to your attention. What you do from here is up to you."

Manipulative jerk. Unfortunately, he wasn't wrong. Ben wasn't going to let a dragon hurt an innocent human woman and Darius knew it. He might not understand it, but he knew it.

"Where is she?" Ben asked, pouring his beer down the sink. No more than a sip for him, since apparently he had to work off the clock now too. And no sleep, either.

Darius waved a hand. "Some frivolous human business establishment. Something to do with animals. Maddox has the address."

CHAPTER 2

Tessa Davelos had her keys out and was reaching for the door to the animal rescue when a half-whispered voice burst out behind her: "You said you weren't coming in to work today!"

Tessa jumped and fumbled the keys. It was Melody, she knew, and she'd been friends with Melody for years, but, damn. Girl could sneak. Tessa was always alert walking from the bus stop to the shelter, and she hadn't even had a clue that Melody was there.

She picked up the keys, turned around, crossed her arms, and stared at her friend.

Melody Keegan was the sort of person who went around looking like the "before" in one of those silly makeover movies the two young women had always made fun of, where the girl takes off her glasses and learns how to dress up and knocks the hero over with her bombshell moves. Mel had long, silky black hair, that Tessa had always secretly envied the hell out of (her own hair was mouse brown), and a pale, china-doll complexion. If Mel would learn to stand up straight, find frames that flattered her face more than those tortoiseshell librarian glasses she wore, and realize that draping herself in shapeless gray sweaters did nothing except turn her naturally hourglass-ish figure into more of a pear, she'd be an absolute bombshell ... as opposed to going around looking like Velma from *Scooby Doo*.

Tessa knew these were not nice thoughts to have about her best friend since high school, but it was a kind of instinctive self-defense mechanism. Mel was a beautiful woman who chose not to be. Tessa knew that she herself was not even pretty. So she'd never bothered trying. She cropped her hair short so as not to deal with it, and she wore shapeless T-shirts to cover up a figure that wasn't even a pear but more of an apple.

And somewhere even deeper down she knew that she shouldn't see it as a competition. It wasn't a competition. It wasn't fair to Mel to think of it that way. But—

But if you don't keep your defenses up, they'll get you.

Whoever *they* were. Girls in school. Foster families. Everyone. The only person she could trust, the only person she had ever been able to trust, was herself. There was nothing special about her, there never had been, except her ability to dig in her (blunt, practical) fingernails and do what needed to be done.

And in this case, enough was enough.

"I can't not come in to work, Mel," she said, sticking the key into the lock. "You can call in sick to the bookstore if you want. I can't. The animals need to be fed."

"I *told* you." Mel's whisper managed to make it all the way to a regular tone of voice, which for her was halfway to a shout. "That thing on your door—"

"You mean that?" Tessa asked, pointing to the vandalized corner of the doorframe. Someone had taken a pocketknife and carved a squiggly thing about six inches high, a winged snake-squiggle. It looked like that thing from the medical staff symbol on ambulances.

Melody's pale complexion went even paler. "Yes, I told you, it's a—a mob symbol. They're going to come after you."

"Because I am marked for death by the mob. Oh no. How will I cope." She started to close the door behind her, but Mel stuck a foot in.

"Tessa, I'm serious. Dead serious. These aren't people you want to mess with."

"Yeah, except I've done absolutely nothing to get on anyone's bad side," she said, even as doubt wormed through her. This was such a strange thing to happen, coming mere weeks after that lawyer had contacted her about her parents. What if—

But no. That was sheer paranoia. Her parents had been an ordinary couple who died in a car crash twenty years ago. A perfectly ordinary car crash. She'd had a long time to get used to it.

"Mel, it was some stupid kid with a pocketknife. I'll sand it out when I get a chance."

"No ... it's not ... aargh!" Melody flexed her hands, opening and closing her fists, and when Tessa tried to shut the door, she ducked inside.

"Look, I'm locking the door, see?" Tessa said, snapping the lock before heading down the hall towards the kennels. A chorus of loud, plaintive cat sounds rose to greet her.

"That won't stop them," Mel complained, tagging along at her heels like an annoying kid sister.

"Oh right, because the mob can walk through walls now?"

"You have no idea," Melody mumbled.

"At least make yourself useful and help me feed the cats."

She had become friends with Melody in high school because they were both weird kids. They weren't really into clothes and makeup the way most of the other girls were, but they weren't part of the gay kids' clique, or the art geeks or the motorheads or the nerds. They were just weird in their own way. So they hung around together, and somehow it turned into a permanent friendship that ended up with the two of them working right across the street from each other, Tessa at a cat rescue and Melody at a bookstore.

But there was a lot about Melody that Tessa had never been able to figure out. Having grown up in foster care herself, she couldn't help being envious of Melody having her parents in her life. And she knew Melody had two living (if divorced) parents. But Melody never talked about her family if she could help it. Tessa had only found out Mel had a half-brother from a few random comments over the years, and she'd never met him.

In a lot of ways, it was like Melody wanted to pretend her family didn't exist. At the same time, she didn't act like anything terrible had happened with them. She didn't seem to hate them or act like she'd been abused. She just didn't want to talk about them.

Or maybe it's just that we were never as close as I wanted to think.

But those thoughts never got her anywhere, and there were chores to do. She got out the cans of wet cat food and handed a bag of dry food to Melody.

"Don't you have work to get to?" she asked.

"The bookstore isn't open yet. Anyway ..." Melody fidgeted, fumbling the open top of the bag and nearly spilling kibble all over the floor. "I'm meeting someone and I told him I'd be here."

Tessa raised her eyebrows. "You've got a date? You've got a date and you told him to meet you at a *cat rescue*?"

"Knock it off, it's not like that."

"Well, if you're gonna be here, then you can clean some litterboxes too."

"Some friend you are," Melody said, with another anxious glance toward the door. "I'm just trying to help."

Her nervousness was starting to make Tessa nervous, and that was going to be transmitted to the cats. She had to get Mel's mind on something else.

"Here, you can pet a kitten. It'll calm you down." Tessa picked up one of the friendliest of the half-grown litter of kittens they were trying to socialize and held it out.

Mel grasped the cat like she was taking a piece of wet laundry. It squirmed, trying to get away. For some reason, animals didn't seem to like Mel; they were nervous around her. It had been that way ever since they were teenagers. Although the way she was holding it certainly wasn't helping.

"Not like that, you have to support its body so it trusts you." Tessa picked up one of the other kittens. "Like this, see? Mel, c'mon, pay attention, it's not like I haven't shown you a thousand times—"

A sudden knock at the door made both women jump, nearly dropping their kittens. Tessa scowled at her friend. It was all Melody's fault, making her this tense. Probably just a shelter volunteer who forgot their keys, or someone who hadn't read their posted hours.

"I'll get it," Melody said quickly, shoving the kitten at Tessa before fleeing down the hall.

"Hey!"

The fact that Mel was now running off to answer the door with no trace of fear made Tessa think there was definitely something going on other than a mob hit (seriously, what *even*). A surprise birthday party? No, her birthday was some months off. She sighed and looked down at the double armload of squirming kittens Mel had left her with. From the hallway, she heard friendly-sounding voices, Mel and a man. Mel's mysterious friend, she guessed.

As the voices came down the hall, Tessa turned, juggling

her armful of kittens. "Say, Mel, if your friend's here, you don't have to stick—around—"

She had never seen this guy before in her life. She definitely would have remembered.

It was like being punched right in the primitive hindbrain, in a way that completely bypassed her conscious mind and went straight to *I would climb that like a tree.*

He wasn't enormously over-muscled, but he was *built*, broad shoulders filling out his charcoal-colored shirt, worn with no tie, with a dark jacket over the top. His black hair showed the faintest trace of silver at the temples—she guessed he was in his late thirties or so—and his eyes were gray, stormcloud eyes focused on her with startled intensity.

Inside her chest, it almost seemed as if something unfurled its wings, an odd little tingling flutter.

And here *she* was, giving this gorgeous guy his first sight of her with an armful of unruly kittens and her hair dried into spikes from this morning's shower, wearing an oversized T-shirt that said ASK ME ABOUT MY CAT HABIT.

"Tessa!" Mel said, oblivious to all of it. "This is my brother Ben. He's going to be your bodyguard for awhile. Because of the—the mob thing?"

Sudden, massive irritation overwhelmed all the conflicting emotions she was feeling. "What the *hell*, Melody? You didn't think you should consult me about this?"

Ben cleared his throat. Now that Melody mentioned it, Tessa could see the family resemblance, at least in their general coloring: dark hair, gray eyes, a fine, clear complexion. There *was* a slight echo of Melody in his chiseled features, though much more masculine and less delicate.

"Ms. Davelos—" he began.

"Stop right there, mister." Though she couldn't help noticing what a nice voice he had, a soft tenor with a slightly

13

gravelly undertone. "I don't want a bodyguard. I don't need a bodyguard. I definitely can't *afford* a bodyguard—"

"Tessa, you're not listening—" Melody began.

"Ms. Davelos, I'm a police officer—" Ben started to say.

"Oh great, you called the *cops*! Just—what is wrong with you, Melody?" Tessa set the kittens gently on the nearest cat tree; *they* at least hadn't done anything to annoy her.

"Tessa, just listen!" Melody's voice was almost a wail, at least as close as she ever got. "You're in danger, terrible danger!"

"From *what*? You keep telling me that, but you won't explain." She glared between the two of them, all too aware that now Mel's hot brother was getting to see her flushed with fury. "If I'm really in danger for some reason, just *tell* me."

"Dragons," Mel's brother said succinctly. Mel's mouth dropped open. So did Tessa's. "You're in danger from dragons."

"Ben!" Mel burst out.

"As Dad's fond of reminding me, I'm not bound by your rules. You might not be able to tell her, but I can." Ben turned to face Tessa. "Ms. Davelos, you're being hunted by a dragon."

Tessa finally managed to scrape enough of her wits together to say, "Get. Out."

"This is why we don't tell people," Mel told Ben between her teeth in a loud, angry whisper.

"Out! Both of you!" Tessa's eyes stung. She'd thought Melody was the one person who would never engage in stupid grade-school pranks with Tessa Davelos as the butt of the joke. (*What's the matter, Pieface? Why aren't you laughing?*) That's what she got for trusting someone. For trusting anyone. "Are you the one who vandalized my doorframe too? What kind of game are you playing? Get *out*!"

Mel flinched away from her, conflict-avoidant to the last,

and some slightly calmer part of Tessa told her, through the hot rage, that none of this made sense. Childish jokes weren't Mel's style, and her fear had seemed to be genuine. Why would Mel make Tessa angry on purpose, when Mel hated people being angry with her? Nothing made sense!

So why won't you tell me the truth? Why these stupid lies about dragons?

She moved forward to push Ben toward the door. Instead he caught her hands. He was shockingly strong, though his grip was gentle.

"I know how you're feeling, Ms. Davelos, but believe me, the threat is real."

"Everyone keeps telling me that, but no one will tell me what this threat actually is!" She wrenched her hands to free herself. Ben was definitely strong enough to have kept holding on, but he let go immediately.

"Can we talk?" He kept his voice calm, his hands out with palms open, eyes on her. "Is there a break room or something similar in here? We could have a cup of coffee and discuss this."

"I'll just be going, then—" Mel began in her whispery voice, starting to duck past her brother into the hallway.

Ben's hand shot out and caught her wrist. "Oh no you don't." He turned to her, and Tessa saw a flash of older-sibling irritation in his gray eyes. "If you and Dad are going to involve me in this, you're gonna stick around to help." He turned back toward Tessa, still holding his sister by the wrist. "Ms. Davelos, none of this is your fault. Just hear me out. Let me explain." With another annoyed glance at Mel: "Both of us will explain."

"An explanation would be very nice, yeah." Tessa tried to stop her voice from shaking. She took a couple of deep breaths and held out her armload of cats. "And if you're going to stay, make yourself useful and pet a kitten. Both of you."

The Keegan siblings stared at her, looking very much alike in that instant. Two pairs of wide, startled gray eyes regarded her in disbelief.

"No kitties," Tessa said, "no talkies."

Melody gave a little huff. "Okay ... fine ..." She took one of the kittens, this time trying to hold it as Tessa had showed her. That didn't help; it still tried to crawl out of her arms as usual.

The other one, though, the one Tessa was still holding ...

To Tessa's surprise, it was struggling in her arms, not to get away, but to go *toward* Ben. He held out a hand, and the kitten scrambled out of her arms and into Ben's. It snuggled up against his chest and started purring.

"Whoa." She glanced over at the one Melody was holding. It was trying to do the same thing, struggling to get out of Melody's arms and crawl onto Ben. "Are you, uh—some kind of natural cat person or what?"

"Something like that." Ben was holding the kitten absently, not paying much attention to it. It didn't seem to care; it snuggled up against him like it had found a long-lost family member.

The high-pitched yowling of the other kittens caught her attention. They were pawing at the wire mesh of their pen, trying to climb through like they, too, wanted to share in some of the petting. Which they'd *never* done before. They were friendly enough with the shelter workers they were familiar with, but nothing at all like this.

And then she realized the rest of the cats in the room were acting weird, too.

One reason why she'd noticed the yowling of the kittens was because the rest of the cats had become strangely hushed. Some of the younger and newer ones were acting like the kittens, fawning against the front of their kennels, wanting attention—even a couple of ferals who had never made a move toward human interaction before. But most of the rest had settled down cautiously, sitting at the fronts of their kennels, and were staring at Ben.

She'd never seen them react to a new person in the kennel room like this before. The shelter had a couple of volunteers who were especially good with them (and one lady who claimed to be a cat whisperer, although Tessa had never notice any sign that communication was actually taking place). But this was something else. It made the hairs on the back of her arms stand up.

Unlike the cat whisperer, Ben didn't seem to be doing anything to attract the cats' attention. In fact, he looked deeply uncomfortable, like someone who had accidentally wandered onstage and had found themselves the unwilling target of attention from a whole room full of people.

Well ... it would be easier to feed them if they were all calm. Except for the kittens, who were going out of their minds. Tessa opened their kennel door and they spilled out to rub around Ben's ankles.

She might not believe in dragons, but there was still something weird about this guy. Aside from the fact that he was almost supernaturally good-looking. Even covered in kittens. *Especially* covered in kittens.

"I'm going to go ahead and finish my morning routine before the shelter opens," she said, wrenching her gaze away. "If you two want to talk, follow along and kitten-wrangle. Pick up a can of cat food if you want. But I'm going to be working."

And the mental image of Ben Keegan covered in adorable kittens was definitely *not* going to be keeping her company while she did that.

Not at all.

17

CHAPTER 3

S he was his mate. His mate!

He didn't know whether to be thrilled or utterly dismayed. He couldn't tell if she liked him at all. At this of all times, his ability to read people seemed to have completely deserted him. He'd never met anyone as inscrutable as Tessa Davelos.

Surely she must feel what he was feeling, or something like it: the tug in his chest every time he looked at her, as if a fishhook had been set behind his breastbone and was pulling him steadily, inexorably toward her.

Did Dad know?

He couldn't have. Shifters couldn't recognize each other's mates. At least Ben didn't think so. *He* couldn't. Maybe dragons could. And his dad was definitely the sort who *would* interfere in his kids' love life ...

But, no. She was his mate. They were fated to meet. If it hadn't been here and now, it would have been somewhere else.

Also, she was marked for death by dragons, and she didn't

even believe dragons existed. That was going to put a defi-
nite damper on the relationship.

"Please take this," Melody muttered between her teeth,
thrusting her unhappy kitten in his direction.

Ben took the kitten absently and let him settle down with
the little girl-kitten already snuggled to his chest. His
panther purred, contented at both the unexpected presence
of his mate and of an armload of cat-children. The kittens
purred back.

Apparently dragons were not nearly as much to their
liking. He noticed a ripple of discontent among the cats as
Melody trailed him, and he followed Tessa, through the
room full of cages.

Tessa worked briskly and busily, scooping out catboxes
and spooning wet food into bowls. After watching for a
minute, Melody picked up a cat litter scoop and went to work.
Ben would have liked to, but his arms were full of kittens and
every time he tried to put them down, they started crying.

Which probably wasn't helping impress his mate that he
was either good mate material or good protector material.
He couldn't even boss around a kitten, for pete's sake.

On the other hand, cats were famously hard to give
orders to. At the moment, most of the cats in the shelter—
aside from the kittens, who apparently had decided he was
their new mom—were regarding Ben and his panther with
wary respect, shaded with a certain element of "What are you
looking at, asshole?"

"I can't believe you just *told* her," Melody muttered out of
the corner of her mouth. "What's wrong with you?"

"What did *you* tell her?" he whispered back.

"That the mob's after her."

"Oh yeah, that's plausible."

"More plausible than dragons!" she shot back.

"I can hear you whispering over there," Tessa said loudly. She straightened up, bag of cat litter in one plastic-gloved hand and a sack of waste in the other. She was utterly gorgeous, scruffy hair and oversized T-shirt and all. She should be a painting: *Woman holding cat litter no. 12.* Her skin was a beautiful caramel color, her hair dark mahogany brown. Ben just wanted to rest his eyes on her forever.

Instead he forced himself to look away, gaze drifting to one of the cats, who stared back, unimpressed, as if to say, *You're not doing a very good job of this so far, buddy.*

"This isn't an easy thing to explain, Ms. Davelos," he said.

Tessa tossed the bag into a bin. "Well, so far, you're not even *trying* to explain."

She had a point. He looked back at her, meeting her deep chocolate-brown eyes. She looked wary, and he was suddenly aware of how much of her defensiveness was a facade. She was worried, scared, and all he wanted to do was put his arms around her and tell her that everything was going to be all right.

Which was the one thing he couldn't do. She was human; she didn't know about fated mates. She didn't know *him.* As far as she was concerned, he was some weirdo who showed up out of nowhere and started babbling about dragons.

And how much reassurance could he offer her? He couldn't take on a dragon and win. In a head-to-head fight, a panther was going to lose.

One thing at a time, though. First he had to get her on board with the idea that the threat was real.

"I know it sounds crazy," he said. "All I can tell you is, dragons exist. And that mark on your doorframe—is it just here, or at your home also?" Maybe they weren't after her; maybe the target was someone else at the shelter, a fellow shifter—

"It's at her home too," Melody said. "Beside her apartment door."

"Kids," Tessa said. "Gang symbols."

Ben shook his head. "That's a dragon symbol. They've marked you. But *why*? The only reason why dragons would come after you like this is if you've trespassed against them. And they wouldn't call out an assassin for a minor offense. It must be something extreme. But from what you've said, you didn't even know that dragons existed until today."

"I still don't know that dragons exist," Tessa said. "You haven't provided a shred of evidence."

Ben glanced at Melody. She gave her head a tiny shake. Great. Not that he'd expected her to agree to shift in front of a human. Dragons were even more secretive than most shifters. Still, it would've been nice to get a little help here.

There was only one other thing to do. It was the last thing in the world he wanted to do. But he had to get her to take the threat seriously. His mate's life was at stake.

"I can give you some evidence," he said. "Not about dragons, exactly. But it ought to help. Are there any cameras in here? Any kind of monitoring?"

Tessa frowned. "*That's* an ominous question if I ever heard one."

"Just tell him, Tess," Melody said.

"There's a kitten webcam in their cage." Tessa pointed to it. "We're far outside its field of view right now, though, and it doesn't pick up sounds. Look, I'm giving you a lot of trust here, buddy, not to just kick you out the door. The fact that you're Mel's brother is the only reason why you're still in here at all." But there was something odd in her voice, a slight hitch as if some part of her wanted to insist otherwise.

"This'll be quick," Ben said. "I'm going to need to take my clothes off. Are we likely to be interrupted in the next few minutes?"

"... wait, you need to *what*?"

Ben set down the kittens carefully and began to undress.

∽

Tessa stared as Ben shrugged out of his jacket. She darted a quick, baffled glance at Melody, but her best friend merely looked exasperated, as if taking his clothes off in public was something her brother did all the time.

"What are you *doing*?" Tessa's voice rose to a startled squeak. Under the jacket he was wearing a shoulder holster, the leather strap cutting a sharp line across pecs that were defined even through his shirt. He carefully unbuckled the holster and hung it on the door of an empty kennel, out of reach of animals or children.

"I could do this without stripping, but I'd ruin my clothes and have nothing to wear afterwards." He unbuttoned his shirt. As Tessa got her first glimpse of his firm, muscular chest, her higher brain functions started to shut down. "You can look away if you want. I wouldn't do this except I really need to convince you, and I can't think of any other way."

Tessa told herself she could stop him. She *should* stop him. All she had to do was say the word and, she thought, he'd stop. And they were getting closer to the shelter's opening time. Other employees and volunteers would arrive soon. Her supervisor might walk in on this.

He stripped out of his shirt, and at that point, she couldn't have looked away if she'd wanted to. The bag of cat litter in her hand dropped to her feet, all but unnoticed. Oh God, he was *built*. Not heavy and overmuscled, but she preferred her men a little bit on the lean side anyway, well defined and strong.

Melody turned away with her hands over her face. "We are never talking about this, Ben. Ever."

"Go guard the door, would you?" Ben suggested with a hint of laughter in his voice.

Melody fled the room.

Ben leaned down to untie his shoes, stepping out of them one at a time, and tucking each of his socks into its respective shoe. The precision intrigued her; most men would've just carelessly dropped their socks on the floor. More distracting, however, was the long curve of his spine, the hint of the top of his ass above his waistband when he bent over ...

He dropped his pants and stepped out of them. Tessa's throat was dry as he hooked his fingers into the waistband of his boxers.

"You can look away," he reminded her.

She didn't look away.

The boxers followed the pants, and then he stood naked before her.

He was *gorgeous*. Now she could see why he moved with such supple grace, with those chiseled muscles and not a speck of extra fat on him anywhere. His chest was lightly furred, dark curls trailing in an enticing line across his flat abdomen, down to the area that she was resolutely *not* looking at—well, maybe a peek wouldn't hurt—

She had to be blushing like a sunrise as she jerked her gaze upward to meet his gray eyes. To her surprise, he was blushing a little too, but then he smiled. "I hope this doesn't shock you too much," he said.

And changed.

Tessa let out a tiny shriek and jumped backward.

It happened almost instantly, though not quite; there was a flowing moment of transition, and she got a brief impression of ink bleeding into his pale skin, of Ben bending forward, and then—

And then the man was gone, and a glossy black panther stood where he had been.

He was the biggest cat she'd ever seen. Certainly the biggest one she'd been next to. This was the jungle prototype of the little house pets in the cages, several hundred pounds of wiry muscle under a coat of gleaming black fur. He was all strength and wildness in a cage of muscle, and her own lack of fear surprised her. Beyond the initial shock, she felt nothing but wonder.

Yellow half-moon eyes gazed into hers, until she was distracted by the sound of a room full of cats going nuts.

As always with cats, there were as many different opinions as there were cats in the room. Some of them were hissing and snarling, puffing up their tails like raccoons. One big, dominant tom cat was clawing at the bars of his cage, trying to get to the panther. Others merely licked their paws and affected a nonchalant air: *Oh, a panther? Must be Tuesday.* Some rubbed on the bars in an attempt to get him to notice them, purring and making little mewling sounds.

The kittens had gone absolutely wild, fawning on him in raptures of delight. Tessa could hear their tiny purrs from where she was standing. Ben became aware of this and looked as confused as a panther could look, staring down at his miniature fan club in feline bafflement.

Tessa's cat-rescue-trained instincts made her hurry forward to remove the little cats from the big cat—you didn't just put strange cats together like this, especially when one of them was huge! ... Except, he *wasn't* a cat, not really, was he? Somewhere in there, he still must have Ben's human mind. And he didn't seem to mind the kittens at all. After his initial moment of surprise, he rubbed his big head against them, knocking some of them over. The kittens didn't seem to mind in the slightest; they were rubbing on him so vigorously that they kept knocking *themselves* over, then scrambling back to their tiny paws for another go at it.

It was the most adorable thing she'd ever seen. Tessa was laughing so hard she could barely speak. "Come on, you silly little things, stop bothering the nice man—er—panther." She picked up a kitten in each hand. They mewed in distress, struggling to escape and go back to their panther lovefest.

Suddenly there was a naked man on hands and knees on the floor, with kittens rubbing all over his wrists. The kittens tumbled all over themselves in shock, and Ben straightened up quickly, reaching for his pants. He cleared his throat. "So."

"So," Tessa echoed. The laughter had died in her throat and now she was just standing, looking at him, with a kitten in each hand.

"Now you know why I was willing to accept that there are dragons after you." He spoke quickly, looking down and concentrating on dressing—avoiding her gaze, she thought with a spark of regret. "There is real magic in the world, Tessa. It's not always friendly."

Tessa opened her mouth to reply, but just then Melody's voice floated down the corridor to them. "Oh hi! No, I just stopped by to visit my friend Tessa. She's back in the cage room—"

"One of the other volunteers is here!" Tessa looked around wildly, with her hands full of kittens. "Put your shirt on!"

"I am!" He looked up from toeing into his shoes and gently removed a kitten from his laces. "Will you let me explain the rest of it?"

"Not in front of my co-workers! They'll think I'm nuts."

"You are in grave danger, Tessa. I don't want to leave you."

"We'll—we'll tell them you're a volunteer, then," she said quickly. "You can fill out the paperwork and help me this morning, and then ... I guess when we get a chance, you can explain the rest to me, and we can figure out what to do next. Okay?"

He smiled, and it was all the more panty-melting now that she'd seen what he looked like with his clothes off. "Okay," he said.

Spending the morning with him wasn't going to be a hardship in the slightest.

Danger, Tessa, she warned herself. She didn't need to be giving her heart away to anyone, no matter how hot he was, no matter the impossible magic that he brought into her world.

If she needed a reminder of how uncertain life could be, all she had to do was touch her chest, where a simple crystal pendant on a silver chain—one of the only things she had left to remind her of her dead parents—rested against her skin beneath her T-shirt.

Life was uncertain and terrible. Things could happen in an instant ... like a car crash. She wasn't going to trust this Ben Keegan guy, no matter how convincing he was.

And she certainly wasn't going to fall in love with him.

CHAPTER 4

Ben spent the morning shadowing Tessa in the animal rescue. Melody, needing to get to her own bookstore job, had left as soon as the other volunteers started showing up—though not without a whispered argument with Ben in the entryway. "I could really use your help if it comes down to a fight with a dragon," he whispered. "Take a day off. Or two."

"I *want* to help, but I can't. You know that! That's why Dad went to you!"

"I don't know why draconic honor is more important than your best friend's life."

"It's not like that. It's honor, it's the clan, it's who we *are*. I thought you'd understand, Ben."

"Yeah, well," he said, his voice tight, "as the dragons in the family keep reminding me, I'm not one of you."

Melody looked up at him with sad gray eyes. "You'll always be one of us."

"Try telling that to Dad." It came out harsher than he intended, and he sighed. Despite the years of sibling rivalry that lay between them, despite the fact that her shifter animal could have easily taken his in a fight, she was still his sister; he hated feeling as if they were on opposite sides in this. "Look, can you help some other way? Do some research, maybe, and see if you can find a loophole that'll help get Tessa out of this? That seems like the kind of thing that's right up your alley."

"Oh, yes! I can do that. I'll get right on it." She smiled up at him. "You're a good man, Ben. I might not be able to protect Tessa, but I know she's safe with you."

Well, that made exactly one of them.

Despite the threat of a dragon assassin showing up, and despite his aching tiredness from having worked a full night before coming down to the shelter, there was no way spending a morning with Tessa could be anything other than pleasant. She gave him a volunteer form to fill out in the shelter's small office while she did paperwork. His mind kept wandering—which he could easily blame on the lack of sleep the night before, but really it was Tessa, just one desk away, and the luscious curves filling out her T-shirt.

He'd never reacted to a woman this way before. (*Well, of course you haven't,* his panther purred. *She's our mate!*) He couldn't get his mind off her, couldn't stop noticing her. All the little things about her: the way she stuck the tip of her tongue out of the corner of her mouth when she was concentrating, the crinkle in her nose when she laughed, the little "V" of close-cropped hair on the back of her neck when she bent her head over her work. He'd never had any particular feelings about short hair on women one way or another (he figured people could do whatever they wanted with their own heads) but her tousled brown hair was simply ... perfect.

She was perfect. Perfect in every way. He loved her soft curves, loved the way her elbows dimpled when she stretched out her arms, loved the hollow of her throat and the glint of a silver chain, just under the collar of her T-shirt, against her light brown, café-au-lait skin ...

"Are you watching me?" Tessa asked, raising her head.

"I was just ... wondering where to put my form."

"Here, I'll take it." She stretched and got up. Ben managed not to stare, but he couldn't help thinking about those perfect round breasts in his hands, stroking her nipples and teasing gasps of pleasure from her throat—

Down, boy.

"What do you want me to do?" he asked quickly, looking for something else to fix his mind on, other than his growing arousal. "I'm not sure what volunteers do in a place like this."

"Oh, lots of things. Clean cages, sort through donations of cat toys and food, help match new cat-parents to find just the right cat for them ... but for you, I have the perfect assignment." She crooked her finger at him. "Come this way."

No arguments here. Anywhere she wanted to go, he'd go.

They went back to the cage room, where a high-pitched chorus of mewling cries greeted them. Tessa opened the kittens' cage and they spilled out into her arms.

"Here," she said, passing Ben an armful of squirming fluff. "Socializing the cats is actually one of the most important jobs our volunteers do." Her eyes sparkled at him. "So that's your job for today. Socializing kittens."

"It'll be difficult," Ben said, deadpan, as the kittens tried to climb his shirt and left stray orange and white hairs all over it, while his panther basked happily in the attention. "But I guess I'll manage."

～

Kittens or not, he tried to stay close to Tessa, causing her to glare over her shoulder at him when he carried the kittens into the office. "Do you have to follow me everywhere?" she asked.

"Do you really want to be caught off guard if—" He broke off; one of the other volunteers was in the office, typing on a computer. "If something happens?" he whispered.

"Do you want everyone I work with to think you're stalking me?" she whispered back, pulling a ledger off a shelf.

"I could go and guard the door instead—"

"No, no, that's worse." She tucked the ledger under her arm and absently grabbed one of the kittens just before it toppled off his elbow as it made a break for freedom. "Let's take this back to the break room. It's less cramped and there shouldn't be anyone there at this time of day."

There wasn't. She spread out the ledger on the table, and Ben took a peek over her shoulder. It was a book of cats. Cats in the shelter, he guessed. Each page had a photo and some notes underneath.

"Do you mind if I ask what you're doing?" he asked, catching a kitten before it could toddle off the table, and trying not to notice how good she smelled.

She flipped a page and scribbled a note on a piece of paper. "I'm looking for good matches between cats and forever homes."

"What does that mean?"

"It means, when someone comes in or calls us looking for a cat, we interview them about what they're looking for, and try to find a good fit for them."

Ben turned his head to take a look at the page she was looking at. It had a picture of a stately-looking Siamese, gazing regally at the camera. "Is there really that much to it?"

"We don't just shove a cat into the hands of every rando

who walks in. We need to get a feel for what kind of owner they'd be and what sort of environment we're sending the cat into. Things like, do they have other pets? Do they have kids? Do they have the time to litter-train and socialize a kitten, or would they prefer an adult cat? Do they want a playful cat, or one who'll sit quietly on their lap? That sort of thing."

"You're right," he said. Distracted from the book, he'd found himself watching the subtle play of light through her dark-brown curls as she spoke. "There's a lot more to it than I knew."

"You're staring at me again."

"Sorry," he said, and bent down to detach two of the kittens from his shoelaces. They really seemed to like those.

"I don't mind," she said quietly.

Ben straightened up quickly, but she'd already risen from the table and went over to the coffee machine, where she rinsed two of the mismatched assortment of mugs in the sink and poured two cups of coffee. "Take anything in it?" she asked over her shoulder.

"Sugar, no cream."

"Hey, me too! Coffee twins." She brought two cups of coffee and a basket of sweetener packets to the table. "I'd have guessed the opposite for you, though. Aren't cats supposed to like cream?"

"Depends on what kind."

He winced as soon as the words were out of his mouth. He'd been going for suave. That was more like "bad pickup line at a bar." But she grinned, giving her a quick flash of her teeth. She didn't smile like that much, with her whole mouth and her eyes; it knocked the breath out of him when she did it.

"You're cute when you're flustered," she said, and shoved the basket of sweetener across the table at him. One of the

31

kittens promptly fell into it. Another sniffed at the coffee cup and toddled away sneezing.

"I feel as if I'm being buttered up for something." He smiled. "Keep doing it. It's working."

She called us cute! His panther preened.

Her smile widened, and she did that little nose-wrinkle thing. "You promised to tell me more about the dragon situation. If anyone comes in, I'm just working on these files while we have a cup of cof—whoa, catch that one!"

With lightning-fast feline reflexes, Ben retrieved a kitten that had been about to wander off the end of the table, and restored it to the purring heap in his lap. Most of them had worn themselves out by now, leaving him with a furry lapful of drowsy, purring kittens.

"I'm going to be lucky if I don't end up with an apartment full of cats at the end of this, aren't I?"

"Occupational hazard," Tessa said, her lips twitching. "So. Tell me about dragons."

"That's a broad topic."

"Okay, let's narrow it down. Tell me what it is about dragons that makes them carve marks in my door and send assassins after me."

He just wanted to go around to her side of the table, put his arms around her, and hold her close. Stopping himself, staying on his side of the table, was almost physically painful. He tried to focus on the situation, not on her nearness and warmth.

"They're old, secretive, and highly honorable. Dragons are easily offended, but they also have a lot of rules about fair fights, and fighting weaker opponents is a violation of their sense of fair play. There's no reason why a dragon would go after a human like this—uh, you are human, right?"

Tessa raised her eyebrows. "As far as I know. And I've known me all my life, so I'm pretty sure, yes."

"Do you have any idea, any at all, why they might be after you?"

"Of course I don't!" she burst out, provoking complaining mewls from the kittens. "I didn't even think dragons were real until a couple hours ago, and I'm still not convinced. How could I offend someone I've never even met?"

"That's what I'm hoping you'll tell me." He kept his voice calm, his interviewing-the-witness voice, even though all he wanted to do was throw himself with fangs and claws at anyone who threatened her. "Can you think of any recent incidents, any enemies that you have—"

She was shaking her head. "I don't have any enemies. I mean, not except the ordinary kind. You could go talk to some of my fourth-grade bullies if you want."

Oh, we'd love to talk to them, his panther growled.

He forced himself not to react. "What about any strange encounters? Has anything odd happened lately?"

"You mean other than this?" she asked dryly. "Nope, no old fortune tellers or dark mysterious strangers ... except for you."

We aren't a stranger, we're her mate!

You, Ben told his panther, *are not helping.*

Aloud, he said, "What about your family? Besides the honor thing, dragons are very focused on family, and they tend to assume the actions of one represent the actions of all. Perhaps someone in your family—"

She was already shaking her head. "Let me stop you before you go any further down that dead-end street. I'm an orphan. I don't even have any close relatives."

"Oh," he said. "I'm—"

"Don't say 'sorry.' That's the worst. It was a long time ago and it's not like it was your fault anyway." She hooked a finger into the silver chain around her neck and tugged on it. "The only thing I have left of my parents is this necklace."

33

There was a pendant on the silver chain, a single clear crystal, about an inch long. She cupped it in her palm and held it out. Ben reached out and cupped his hand under hers, lifting it to see better. Her skin felt very warm, and he was acutely aware that the pendant had just been tucked into her cleavage.

"Could this be magic in some way?" he asked, tilting her hand so it caught the light.

Her fingers jerked in his. "*What?*"

"It could be why the dragons are after you."

"It's just a rock," she protested. "These are a dime a dozen in any New Age store. Maybe my mom was a hippie or something. I don't even know if it's a family heirloom, because they're not around to ask. It's certainly not magic."

"Are you *sure?*"

CHAPTER 5

Was she sure?

Tessa tilted her palm, Ben's hand moving under hers, and watched the pendant sparkle at the end of its chain. She'd first seen it two weeks ago, when the package from the lawyer arrived in the mail, containing a box of her parents' effects.

I'm sorry it took me so long to locate you, Ms. Davelos. My instructions were to deliver this to you when you turned 21, but after your parents' deaths you went into the foster care system, and proved difficult to track down ...

But there hadn't been anything expensive in the box, no family diamonds or secret treasure maps. It was stuff that her parents had thought important enough to put in a safe deposit box with the law firm, but it was just family papers: their marriage license and birth certificates, some family photos, and this necklace. If the necklace was valuable, she couldn't tell. Perhaps it was merely of sentimental value and her mother had wanted to give it to her when she was older.

It had meaning to her because it was all she had left of the parents she'd never had a chance to know. That was all.

But before this morning, she'd have said it was impossible for a guy to turn into a panther. It was impossible for dragons to exist. It was impossible for a blazing hot guy with gorgeous gray eyes to walk into the shelter and turn her world upside down ...

She blinked and forced herself to look away from the pendant, and away from the stormcloud eyes gazing into hers. "It's not magic," she said "It's just a cheap trinket."

"If you say so," he said, which surprised her. She was expecting more of an argument. She wasn't used to being taken at her word like that.

"You believe me?"

He smiled. "I believe you haven't been given any reason to think it's magical. That's enough for me."

His hand was still cupped under hers, cradling her fingers in his palm. He'd leaned across the table to look more closely at the pendant, which meant his face was practically in her cleavage. She could smell his spicy, clean male scent, with light overtones of aftershave and shampoo.

Desire curled through her, pooling in her belly. Just being this close to him was sweet torment. She wanted to have his lips on hers, wanted to feel the touch of his firm body pressed against her own; it was like something was pulling her toward him, an undertow she had to keep struggling against.

She was less and less sure that she wanted to fight it at all.

Making a final effort to regain some personal space, she cleared her throat and pulled her hand out of his. He let her go, though his fingers brushed along the edge of hers, setting off answering sparks all up and down her nervous system. She looked away as she stuffed the pendant back into her T-shirt, but all that did was make her realize that he'd been getting a nice view down the top of her shirt into her cleavage.

Not that she minded.

It was increasingly difficult to concentrate on anything except her growing arousal. Her fingers felt cool where his hand had pressed, missing the warmth of his skin.

"I think these little guys are asleep," Ben said quietly, returning his hand to his lap where the kittens were nestled.

"Oh yeah ... yeah, let's put them back in their kennel for awhile."

She got up quickly and helped him with his kitten load, taking two of them out of his lap and trying very hard not to think about her own proximity to—Okay, kittens. Thinking about kittens.

"I keep thinking I should have done this before," Ben said as she put the kittens back on their soft blanket in their kennel, one by one.

"Done what before?" He was so close to her; their arms and hands brushed each time she took a kitten from him. "Protected young ladies from dragons? Does that make you a knight?"

His smile was warm and made his eyes crinkle. "No. Volunteered at an animal shelter. I've always gotten along well with cats, but my life is too busy for a pet. I never realized that I could just come in and ..."

"Cuddle some kittens?" she asked softly, taking the last little bit of orange fluff from his hands.

"Yeah."

His fingers lingered on hers. She found that her hand wanted to curl around his; her fingers wanted to nestle in his palm as the kittens had done. No wonder the kittens liked him, trusted him. She felt the same, an instinctive trust for him, as if her soul and his had already met in a past life ... or were fated to meet in this one.

He was handsome and strong and protective, and he

loved cats. Heck, if she hadn't been hallucinating earlier, in some sense he *was* a cat.

Why the hell was she fighting this so hard?

"Tessa," he murmured, and she tilted her head back and gave in to the longing pulling her toward him.

His lips crashed onto hers. She leaned into him, opening her mouth into his, sliding her arms under his jacket to run her hands up and down the smooth plane of his back. A single kiss wasn't enough; she just wanted more, more, *more*.

It was like she'd been offered her first drink of water after a lifetime's thirst.

Their hands were all over each other; she sensed the same hunger, the same thirst in him. When she drew back, his pupils were blown, and he gazed at her with open wonder.

"That was—" she began.

"Amazing," he breathed.

And just then the door to the cage room opened, and one of the other volunteers leaned in. "Tessa? There's a—oh." She paused. "Sorry."

"Everything's fine," Tessa said quickly, as Ben straightened his shirt. "Did you need me for something?"

"There's someone outside to see you. He doesn't want to come in, and he didn't give a name."

Tessa was aware of Ben, at her shoulder, somehow becoming fiercer and more menacing, as if she could sense the panther in him. Some of the cats hissed.

"I'll be out in a minute," she called, and as soon as the other volunteer left, she smacked Ben in the chest with the back of her hand. "Cool it. It's probably just someone interested in volunteering. You don't really think a dragon assassin is going to try to murder me in broad daylight surrounded by witnesses, do you?"

"I don't know what he's capable of." Ben reached under his jacket to touch his gun. "Stay behind me."

"I'm not a damsel in distress," she scoffed, and marched out of the cage room.

Her bravado faltered as soon as she stepped out onto the street, and suddenly she was very glad of Ben at her back. Because there was something really *not normal* about this guy.

He was quietly leaning a shoulder against the wall near the door to the shelter. She'd never seen him before, but the first word that came to mind to describe him was *sharp*. He wore a black leather motorcycle jacket and his dark hair was swept back from a pointed widow's peak. His skin was a light golden brown; his dark eyes and high cheekbones hinted at, perhaps, some Asian or Native American ancestry. It was a similar racially mixed look to what she saw when she looked in the mirror. Not having known her parents, Tessa wasn't sure about her own ethnic background either; she thought it was probably just a little of this, a little of that.

An odd thought crossed her mind: *could he be related to me?*

But if so, he couldn't be a close relative—they didn't look *that* alike—and anyway, that was the only thing she had in common with this guy. He carried no visible weapons, but he looked dangerous. It was something in the way he carried himself, the balanced grace and confident strength. It was, in fact, very much like the way Ben stood, the way Ben moved.

"Tessa Davelos?" the stranger said, pushing himself off the wall.

Behind her, she felt Ben tense, and then he was shoving her out of the way and stepping in front of her.

The man in the motorcycle jacket tilted his head and looked at them both with a narrow-eyed, appraising stare. "My business is with the young lady. Please stand aside."

"The hell I will." Ben's teeth were bared; he was all but

bristling. If he was a cat, Tessa could tell his fur would've been standing on end. "She's under my protection."

"Hey," Tessa said, sliding out from under his arm. "I can speak for myself, thanks. Who the heck *are* you?"

"My name is Reive," the stranger said, unruffled. "I have to say, you aren't what I was expecting. You're just a little scrap of a thing."

It was probably the first time she'd been called a little scrap of anything. "What were you expecting?" Tessa asked, baffled.

Ben moved forward, closing on Reive, who stood his ground. "Whatever you want with her, she knows nothing about it. You have no right to come after her, you dishonorable bastard."

The corner of Reive's mouth lifted in a very slight sneer, baring a flash of his teeth. "You speak of dishonor to me, when you are interfering in matters that concern you not at all? Stand aside."

"Ben, be careful," Tessa called.

She looked around anxiously. So far no one was paying much attention—one thing about living in the city, a couple of people having an argument on the sidewalk was the kind of thing you didn't get involved with.

Should she scream?

But what was she going to say? The stranger in the leather jacket wasn't threatening them in any obvious way. She trusted Ben with a conviction she still couldn't quite understand, but it wasn't like she could yell "Dragon! Help!" and expect people to take her seriously.

"I'm giving you one last chance," Ben said. He'd closed on Reive until the two of them stood face to face, Reive not backing down an inch. They were about the same height, somewhere in the neighborhood of six feet or so. "Turn around. Walk away. Leave her alone."

"Do you know what I am?" Reive asked coolly.

"I know exactly what you are, dragon."

Reive grimaced and glanced past Ben at the oblivious passing shoppers. *That's his weakness,* Tessa thought. *He doesn't want anyone to know about him. And Ben knows it.*

"Then you know that I can't," Reive said, turning his dark eyes back to Ben—unblinking, like the eyes of a snake. "I've been given a task by my clan and I am honorbound to carry it out. I must return to my clan with her mortal remains—"

Ben moved so fast it was unreal; to Tessa he was nothing but a blur. He seized Reive's arm, doubled it behind him, and used that grip to slam Reive into the wall. Reive didn't resist; he seemed too surprised.

"You're under arrest," Ben said flatly.

Reive gave a startled laugh, slightly choked because his head was twisted to the side, cheek pressed against the wall. "*What?*"

"You have the right to remain silent. Anything you do or say—"

"You can't arrest me." Reive's thin lips curved in a slight smile. "Your mortal law has no hold over me. I can escape easily."

"Oh really?" Ben said. "You want to reveal yourself, then? Shift in front of a street full of, as you put it, *mortals?* Let's see you do that, then."

Reive gave a short, hard laugh, but he didn't move as Ben snapped a pair of handcuffs around his wrists. "May I ask what exactly you're arresting me for?"

"You made a death threat against the lady. Right in front of a cop."

"Ah," Reive said.

"Which makes me think you're the one who's been stalking and harassing her. Someone committed vandalism

41

on her door and on the door of the shelter. How about we take a ride down to the station and talk about it?"

Reive turned to look at Tessa. She had to take a step back; it felt as if his cold, hard eyes were boring straight through her. "If you think this is going to make the slightest difference to the outcome," he said quietly, "then you are both fools."

Ben swung Reive around with an expert grip on his cuffed hands and shoulder, holding him firmly. "Ma'am, you want to press charges against this man?" His voice was a gruff cop voice, but his eyes said *Please*.

"Um," Tessa said. "Yes?"

"You heard her. Let's take a ride down to the station. Tessa," he said over his shoulder, "I'll be back in about an hour. Can you be ready to go when I get back?"

"Go where?" Tessa asked. Everything was out of control; her life had turned into a runaway train, and all she could do was stare at the scenery speeding past and wish she had the courage to jump off.

"Yes, go where?" Reive asked nastily.

"Shut up," Ben said, giving him a hard shake. "Tessa, tell your boss you're going to have to take a couple of days off. Family emergency, or—I don't care, make something up. Tell him it's a matter of life and death."

Tessa swallowed. "That's a lot of trust you're asking for," she said.

"I know," Ben said quietly.

"How charming," Reive remarked.

Ben shook him again. "Shut *up*."

But the crazy thing was, she did trust him. She trusted him enough to follow him into the unknown, believing that he would keep her safe.

"Yes, I'll talk to my boss," she said, pushing down her

misgivings. If her life was a runaway train, from here on out she'd chosen to be on it. "Hurry back. I'll be waiting."

CHAPTER 6

"This won't work, you know," Reive said in an infuriatingly calm voice.

"What part of 'right to remain silent' do you not understand? Shut up back there."

Reive was in the back of Ben's car, still securely handcuffed as far as Ben could tell. So far he'd made no attempt to escape. Ben would have been less nervous if Reive had actually tried to escape, or shown any anxiety about being arrested at all. He'd been as calm as if the whole thing was his idea.

"All I have to do is call my clan's attorney. I'll be out in hours."

"Those are hours you won't be threatening her, so I'll call it a win." Ben glanced at him in the rear-view mirror, but Reive didn't seem to be squirming or trying to work on the cuffs. "Are you the only one, or did they send others?"

"I thought I was supposed to remain silent," Reive said, another tiny smile flickering at the corner of his mouth. "In order not to incriminate myself."

"Your lawyer's not here. Piss me off enough, and I'll pull this car over and *make* you answer my questions."

"Really? You want it to come to a physical fight? You know who'd win, right?"

"You might change your mind if I'm pushed into a corner," Ben said between his teeth.

"Oh really? What *are* you, anyway?" Reive leaned forward. "You know about us, so you're no ordinary human. I'd be able to tell if you were a dragon. Are you some kind of shifter?"

"None of your business."

"Hmph." Reive leaned back again. "You want me to answer your questions, but you won't answer mine? Tell you what, a question for a question. You tell me what you are and why you care what happens to that girl, and I'll tell you if I'm the only dragon on her trail."

"Sounds like you're getting the better end of that deal," Ben said tightly.

"Straight swap, then. A question for a question. What *are* you, detective?"

"I'm a panther shifter," Ben said. "Your turn. How many assassins did your clan send?"

"Just me. One is enough." Reive laughed softly. "A cat, are you? How appropriate. The cat, sent to protect the girl who loves cats."

A cold shiver went through Ben; his hands tightened on the steering wheel. "How long have you been watching her, bastard? How much do you know about her?"

"Is that your next question?"

"The thing I really need to know is why you're after her. She's only a human. She doesn't even know about your kind."

"If that's what you think," Reive said, "then she's lying to you."

Ben pulled up in front of the police station with a sharp

45

jab to the brakes, jolting both of them forward in their seats. "She's not lying."

"You sure of that?"

Ben had to forcibly hold back his panther, pacing and furious at the slight to their mate. "What makes *you* say that?"

"No more free answers, kitty cat," Reive said, leaning back. "This is dragon business. Just let us take care of it. You can't beat me in a fight; you *know* that. Panther versus dragon? Don't make me laugh. If you stand aside and let me have the girl, my clan won't hold a grudge."

Ben's panther vibrated with rage, making his hands shake as he manhandled Reive out of the car, not very gently. "You won't lay a finger on her. You won't come near her. If you so much as *look* at her—"

"You'll do what, detective? Kill me? Oh, you *do* have it bad, don't you?"

"You don't know the half of it," Ben growled, propelling him into the police station.

Reive continued to be docile and cooperative during the booking process—suspiciously so, one might think, but Ben knew from dealing with his father that dragons usually *were* polite and cooperative ... right up to the point where they decided they'd been pushed too far, and that was when things got ugly.

But the biggest taboo in dragon culture, as with shifters, was breaking the veil of secrecy that kept them all safe. Ben was about as confident as he could be that Reive wouldn't try to shift in the middle of a police station, and so far it seemed he was right. Reive observed with curiosity as he was finger-printed, and gave his name to the booking officer as Reive Corcoran, spelling it with fastidious precision.

"I'm allowed a phone call, correct?" he asked. "On television, one can make a phone call. I'd very much like to call my lawyer."

Ben couldn't come up with a good pretext for stopping him. Reive was right, his lawyer would have him out in hours. But at least this way, he and Tessa would get a head start.

His father would have laughed at him for trying to solve his problems using human law, human technology. *They can't protect us,* the voice of his father whispered in his head. *We are not like them. We solve our own problems, our way.*

Yeah, maybe that's true, Ben thought as he strode out of the station after arranging a few days' personal leave. *But apparently dragons are powerless to solve Tessa's problems because of their stupid honor. So I'm just going to have to use a little bit of human-style ingenuity to keep her safe.*

It's all I've got.

~

"I'm so sorry," Tessa told her boss on the phone. "It's my mother, she's had a fall—we think she'll be all right, but I have to go out of town for a couple of days."

Inwardly she writhed with guilt. She never even told little white lies, normally. And the worst part was how understanding her boss was about it. As the shelter's adoption coordinator and office manager, she was one of their only paid employees. It might mean having to close the shelter to new adoptions for a little while.

And they were short on volunteers right now, too, she reflected as she hastily updated her records in the hope that the shelter could run smoothly without her for a few days. Normally she took up the slack when their animal-care volunteers were late or absent. The adult cats would be all right for a day or two with dry food and automatic waterers, but the kittens ...

47

They'd probably be okay physically, but they had been trapped as ferals, and they were doing so well at learning to trust and depend on humans. She'd worked so hard on it. Running off and leaving them felt like abandonment.

There was a soft-sided carrier in the shelter's supplies ...

A few minutes later, she was locking the door, with the softly mewing carrier sitting by her feet, a bag of kitten food and other supplies beside it. She'd canceled the next few days' adoption appointments and made the shelter as idiot-proof as it could be for her absence.

"Tessa!"

Melody ran across the street from the bookstore. She'd tied her dark hair up in a bun, as she usually did when she was working; that, combined with her gray cardigan, made her look even more like a stereotypical librarian than usual.

"Are you leaving town?" Melody whispered fiercely as soon as she was close enough. "You believe me now, right?"

"I'm not coming in to work for the next couple of days. Ben is keeping me company."

Melody opened her mouth.

"No stupid innuendos," Tessa said quickly. "We're just friends."

"I think you're a lot more than that," Melody said, and to Tessa's irritation, her friend winked at her.

"Good grief, I know he's your brother, but knock off the matchmaking for one freaking—Oh, hold on a minute—"

In the carrier at Tessa's feet, the kittens' wailing had increased in volume. Their little claws scrabbled on the fabric. Tessa moved the carrier behind her, and they settled down somewhat.

"It's weird that cats hate you so much, when they love Ben," she remarked. Melody looked uncomfortable, and Tessa frowned at her. "Wait a minute. If Ben is—are *you*—"

"Can we not have this conversation on a public street-corner?" Melody hissed, looking around wildly as if she expected a whole crowd of eavesdroppers. In reality, there wasn't anybody nearby.

"Are you a panther too?"

"No!" Melody said. "Keep your voice down!"

"Is this why you never talk about your family?"

"What exactly has Ben told you?" Melody asked. "About his—about *our* parents."

"Not much. We've only known each other for a couple of hours."

Melody looked relieved. "Good. Look, just ... be *careful*, okay? I trust Ben to keep you safe, but you're still in a lot of danger."

"Ben's a cop," Tessa said. "I'm sure he knows a lot about keeping people safe."

"I know." Melody hesitated before giving her friend a quick hug. Tessa, surprised, hugged her back. Neither of the women were really the hugging sort, under usual circumstances.

"Call me and let me know you're okay," Melody said into her ear. "I'm so sorry I can't help more."

"I don't expect you to. You've helped a lot already, hooking me up with Ben." *In more ways than one,* she couldn't help thinking as she let her friend go.

"I know, but—"

A car pulled up to the sidewalk beside them. Tessa's first instinct was a flinch of fear, and she noticed Melody move subtly in front of her, which was touching even if Melody was about as threatening as a pillow. But it was just Ben's car, an unmarked, ordinary-looking sedan. With no handcuffed assassin in the back of it this time, Tessa was relieved to note.

Ben got out wearing sunglasses, which was hot enough to make Tessa's knees go a little weak. Then he pushed the sunglasses up on his head and her knees stayed weak, so maybe it was just Ben.

"Ready to go?" he asked her.

She nodded and picked up the carrier, which squalled in protest.

"Um," Ben said, "that's ..."

"I can't leave them alone at the shelter without me," Tessa said quickly, reaching with her other hand for the bag of kitten supplies. "They're very unobtrusive, you'll never even know they're there—"

The carrier helpfully provided a soundtrack of *MewmewmewmewMWAAAAUUULLL—!*

"Tessa, we aren't—you can't—" Ben raised his hands and then let them drop. "Fine. Put it in the backseat."

"Thank you," she said quickly, shoving the carrier and supplies into the back of the car before he changed his mind.

Ben shoved his hands in his pockets and gave Melody a look that Tessa couldn't quite interpret. "Not going to offer to come with us?"

"I feel like I'd be more help here, doing research like you suggested."

"Probably," Ben said.

"I'll do that, then. But call me if you need anything. I could be your supply drop."

"I hope we won't be gone long enough to need it, but thanks. I'll be in touch."

Melody hesitated, squeezed Tessa's hand, and then ran back across the street to the bookstore. Ben turned to Tessa.

"Do you have a car, or did you take public transportation to work?"

"I don't own a car. I just take the bus."

"Good. That'll make it easier. Let me know how to get to where you live, so you can pack a bag."

It was starting to feel real now. She clenched her hands to

stop them from trembling. "So we really are going out of town?"

"If you're okay with it," Ben said. "I have a place out in the woods. A cabin. It's not in my name. I guess you could call it a sort of bolt hole. There's no way anyone should be able to find us there. You'll be perfectly safe for as long as we like."

The idea of being safe sounded great, but ... "That won't solve anything, though, will it? If they're after me now, they'll still be after me if I go into hiding."

"Yes, but it'll buy us some time." He nodded to the car. "Get in. Let's talk on the way. We're racing a clock; Reive's going to be out of jail as soon as his lawyer can spring him."

Tessa gave him her apartment building's address and clenched her hands in her lap as they drove across town. Ben was calm, at least outwardly, but between his warnings and Melody's, she was starting to see dragons behind every lamp-post. The shadow of a building passing over the car made her jump.

"Hey." Ben reached over and closed his hand over hers, comforting and strong. "It's going to be okay. I'll keep you safe. All right?"

"All right," she whispered, lacing her fingers through his.

∾

At her apartment, Ben waited near the door, studying the mark on the doorframe, while she quickly shoved some clothes into a suitcase. "No cats?" he asked.

"It's a no-pets apartment. Believe me," she said, managing a smile, "as soon as I find a place where I can have cats, I'm going to get one. At least one. Maybe two. Maybe twelve." She balled up some bras and underwear, shoving them into her bag. She hesitated over the box of papers from her parents, but decided to leave it. She'd lived without it all her life; she didn't need to carry a few old family photos around with her. "Okay. Let's go."

"That's it? You can take longer, you know. Take whatever you want. There's room in the car."

"I just needed a change of clothes. There's nothing here I care about." She shrugged. "When you grow up in foster care, you get used to traveling light."

She didn't mean it to come out self-pitying. She was just stating facts! But there was an inescapable vestige of an old and deep pain; she could even hear it in her own voice, the echoes of a lonely child who had carried around all her belongings in a plastic garbage bag. She didn't dare look at Ben. Instead she turned away and took a mug from the sink, filling it with water for the cats.

"Anyway," she said shortly, "let's get on the road."

Ben picked up the suitcase without being asked and, at her nod, carried it down to the car for her. While he put it in the trunk, she leaned a knee on the seat beside the cats' carrier and unzipped the top just enough to get a hand inside. There was no built-in water dish and she realized too late that she'd forgotten to bring something from the apartment. "Do you have something back there I can water them with?"

Ben supplied a plastic coffee-can lid, but the cats were far more interested in trying to crawl out over her hand. She gave up, took the water out to prevent it from spilling, and zipped them back in. "How far is it to this cabin of yours?"

"A couple hours' drive. Will they be okay for that long?"

"They'll be fine." The kittens mewled plaintively, making it clear they did not agree. "You don't mind having cats in your cabin, do you? I forgot to ask."

"I don't mind at all. It's quiet out there with just me. I like quiet, but ..." He smiled at her, crinkling his eyes as they got into the car. "Sometimes you can use a little noise."

She had to look away from the warmth of his eyes. "No pets of your own, right?"

"No. Hard to take care of pets with a cop's hours. Or have a social life, really."

"No girlfriend?" she asked, her throat dry at her own boldness.

"No," Ben said, and smiled at her. "Not yet."

CHAPTER 7

As they drove out of the city, apartment buildings gave way to suburban houses with flowers in their front yards, which gave way eventually to trees and farms. Tessa was fascinated. She'd lived in several different cities and large towns as she bounced around between foster homes, but had rarely been in the country, though she had vague memories of having lived in a small town with her parents as a child, somewhere in the mountains.

They didn't talk much at first. Ben turned the radio on, and Tessa watched the landscape roll past in a thousand shades of green, drinking in its beauty. At one point, Ben pulled off on a little gravel turn-out beside a stream. She looked at him in surprise.

"Are we there already?"

"No, it's just that I saw you looking around and this is one of my favorite places to stop and stretch my legs on the drive. I thought you might want to see it."

The day was warm and still, the air filled with unfamiliar smells. It was so quiet that the rushing water seemed very loud. The traffic was light, only a few cars passing as Tessa knelt beside the stream to look at the rocks.

"Do you really think we're safe from Reive following us?" she asked, looking up at Ben.

"I don't see how he can. I swept the car thoroughly for bugs back at the station, just in case he might've tagged us somehow. And there's no straightforward way to trace the cabin to me. One of my dad's shell companies owns the land."

"Shell companies?"

Ben hesitated. "My dad has his finger in a bunch of different business interests. I figured I might as well take advantage of it for a change."

That was ... cryptic. She decided not to ask about it at the moment; she sensed a lot of history there, and she didn't want to spoil the pleasant mood of the day. It seemed impossible that danger could intrude on this quiet, beautiful spot. When she held out her hand, Ben took it, lacing his fingers through hers. She leaned against him, a pleasant heat flooding her at his nearness.

She hoped the cabin had a comfortable bed, because she had a feeling that by the time they got there, she was going to be aching with how much she wanted him. For a moment she entertained the pleasant fantasy of having him lay her down beside the stream—but no, as well as being right beside the road (and while there wasn't a lot of traffic, there was definitely *some*), she had a feeling that outdoor sex was more fun in daydreams than in bug-filled, rocks-and-sand reality.

"Ready to go?" Ben asked quietly, and she nodded. He pressed a kiss to her temple and they got back in the car.

Now, though the scenery was just as beautiful in the afternoon sun, she found it hard to stop thinking about that sharp-eyed stranger in the leather jacket and the threat he posed. "Did Reive tell you anything about why he's after me?"

Ben shook his head. "No. All I got out of him is that his

clan sent him, and only him. At least we only have one assassin to deal with."

"One's more than enough. Do you think he's telling the truth?"

"Dragons don't usually lie. It's not that they can't, it's just that they don't think it's honorable."

Honor again. She wanted to spit on it. "And a clan, that's like a dragon family, or what?"

"Yeah, basically, or a group of families united under a single leader. Dragon families are very close-knit, but also ..." His voice darkened with a bitterness that puzzled her. "—not very welcoming of anyone they don't consider part of the clan. They don't like outsiders. They don't like other dragon clans much, either. There are a lot of feuds."

"So basically you're saying they're a scaly version of the Hatfields and McCoys."

Startled, he laughed. "Yeah, I guess you could say that."

He slowed and turned off the highway into a small town, its tidy brick buildings framed by the sharp blue peaks of nearby mountains. As they drove slowly through the picture-postcard downtown, Tessa noticed a small, independent bookstore with a GOING OUT OF BUSINESS! sign in the window, and made a mental note to mention it to Melody. She knew her friend enjoyed her job at a chain bookstore outlet, but daydreamed about opening a small used book-store of her own. Space rent in the city was prohibitively expensive. Perhaps a small town like this, with a market niche left unfilled by the bookstore's closing, would be an easier place for Melody to realize her dream.

"We're close now," Ben said. "This is the nearest town to my cabin. It's just a little way out of town, up in the hills." He pointed to a sign reading BROWN BEAR CAFE as they passed it. "My friends Derek and Gaby run that place. If we're here long enough, I'll take you there so you can try

Gaby's amazing strawberry shortcake while it's in season. Best I've ever had. She gets the fruit from a local farm."

"It looks like a nice place to live." Tessa heard the wistfulness in her own voice. She'd never craved small-town life, but she wasn't that fond of the city either, as much as she liked working at the cat rescue. She just wanted a place to belong. A home.

"I like it out here," Ben admitted, turning out of town onto a small side road. "Derek's been trying to talk me into retiring from the force and moving out here to start a bodyguard business with him. He's been doing some security-guard work on the side, to keep himself from getting too bored helping Gaby bake cupcakes."

"Are his cupcakes any good?"

"Not as good as Gaby's strawberry shortcake."

The town fell behind them, and trees closed around the road. It looked like the forest primeval. Serried ranks of pines lined the road, enclosing them in deep green shadows with occasional flickers of sunlight. Something about it tugged at her memory, evoking a faint echo of nostalgia. She might have lived somewhere like this with her parents, once upon a time.

The cats would probably love it out here. She just hoped she could keep them from wandering too far and falling prey to owls or foxes or whatever else hunted these woods.

... which, come to think of it, might include Ben as well. "I hope this isn't rude," she said. "But I was wondering if you ... uh ... go hunting out here? As a panther, I mean."

The question sounded terribly odd to her, but Ben smiled. "Sometimes," he said. "It's one of the benefits of coming out to the woods, being able to shift at will without anyone seeing me."

"Are there many other people like you?" she asked. Now that she'd raised the topic, questions tumbled through her mind. "How does it happen? You weren't, like ... bitten by a panther, or something?"

"No," he said with a smile. "I was born this way. And there are other people like me, but not very many. Like being a dragon, it runs in families."

He stopped abruptly as he finished the sentence, but Tessa's mind had already jumped ahead to the inevitable conclusion. "Melody told me she wasn't a panther. Is that right?"

"It's true," Ben said. "She's not a panther."

There was something a bit strange about the way he said it, as if Melody might not be a panther, but she was something else. Before Tessa could ask about that, though, he made a sharp turn onto a road that was little more than two ruts. She clung to the handle on the inside of the door as they jolted over ruts. Branches scraped the sides of the car.

"I need to get a chainsaw and brush this out," Ben remarked. "I haven't been up here this summer as much as I'd like."

The road, driveway, or whatever it was made a few sharp turns, and then suddenly they came out of the dark, dense trees into a clearing flooded with the soft golden light of afternoon. Ben parked and turned off the engine.

"Home sweet home," he said, and the glance he gave her was oddly shy.

He really likes it here, she thought. *He wants me to like it too.*

But before she could do more than grasp at the thought, Ben opened his door and got out. Sweet-smelling, warm afternoon air flooded the car. After a moment, she followed suit, stretching beside the car.

The cabin was picturesque as a photo in a calendar, two stories tall with a high, peaked roof that had something like a cupola at the top. It stood alone in the center of a meadow. Tessa turned, shading her eyes with her hand, looking across the tall grass, dotted with wildflowers, sweeping away to smoke-blue shadows under the trees. Somewhere nearby, she could hear water rushing in a brook.

"This is the most beautiful place I've ever seen," she said, and meant it.

Ben straightened up from getting her suitcase out of the trunk, smiling. "I'm glad you think so," he said.

His sincerity struck her right to the heart. She wasn't used to having anyone look at her like that, as if her opinion really *mattered*.

"Anyway," he added, "you can get the cats out of their carrier, and I'll make us some lunch. Or more like dinner now, I suppose."

Lugging the cat carrier with its squirming, uncooperative burden, she followed him up the porch and waited while he unlocked the door.

"I haven't been out here in a while, so it might be a little musty inside," he said, opening the door. "Just leave this open to let some air in. I'll throw the windows open too."

"The cats," she began.

"Oh, damn. Sorry. I forgot about that."

"No, it's better if we don't give them the run of the house at first." She looked around the room she'd stepped into. It looked like a combination living room and kitchen, with a fieldstone fireplace and squashy, comfortable-looking couches and chairs. A loft with a railing overlooked the downstairs. There was a sawhorse in the living room, and the whole place smelled of sawdust.

"Sorry about that." Ben shoved the sawhorse against the wall. "I've been doing some work on the place, repairs after we had some issues last summer, and it's still kind of a construction zone. Anyway, there are two bedrooms downstairs." He opened the bedroom doors as he spoke, giving her a glimpse of small rooms with stripped-down mattresses on wooden bedframes. "A third bedroom upstairs is where I normally sleep. And here's the bathroom ..."

Following him, she glanced inside. It was small but clean, with an old-fashioned, claw-foot tub and a shower enclosure.

"You can either put the cats in the bathroom, or one of the bedrooms. I'm not sure which would be better."

"Bedroom, I think. That way we don't need to open the door except to feed them. I'll let them into the main house later, if you're okay with that?" She waited for his affirming nod before she went on. "But right now they're going to be freaked out and probably just want a quiet place to hide. Also, er ... another reason not to give them the run of the main house just yet is that they're still pretty young and might not be fully litter-trained yet in a new environment. Speaking of which, I brought litter with me, but I also need some kind of shallow tray or pan."

"I'll go find something. Is there anything else you need?"

"Food and water dishes?" Tessa suggested.

"I'll see what I can find." He pulled the door shut as he left.

It was cool and quiet in the bedroom. The only furniture was the bed with its bare mattress and a small wooden dresser beside it. Tessa knelt on the bare wood floor to set the carrier down in a shadowed corner between the dresser and the wall.

"It's okay, babies. You can come out now."

She unzipped the carrier and reached in to pet the kittens. Leaving the unzipped side panel open, she sat with her back against the bedframe, giving them the opportunity to explore in their own time. A small orange nose peeked out of the carrier, and then vanished back inside when Ben knocked on the door.

"C'mon in," she called, and he cracked open the door and slipped carefully through. He'd found a plastic bucket lid for a litterbox, and she shook out some litter from the mostly-empty bag she'd brought from the shelter, while Ben put down a bowl of water for the kittens. Tessa put a handful of dry kitten food into the cracked saucer Ben had scrounged as a food dish, but she got no takers when she shook it.

"Are they okay?" Ben asked, sitting on the floor beside her with an arm draped loosely over his knees.

"I think so. They're just shaken up from the trip and not sure about this new place. Oh, look, there they go."

As soon as one of the kittens toddled out into the world, the others followed quickly. Tessa picked up a couple of them and set them in the litterbox to show them where it was—the litter smelled the same as what they used in the shelter; the kittens should recognize it—but they were much more interested in creeping around the edges of the room and exploring under the bed.

There were five kittens: a very small orange one, two larger orange ones, one gray, and one with gray and white spots. In the shelter Tessa had worried that the little orange one would lose out on food and attention to the bigger kitties, but he'd turned out to be pushier than his bigger brothers and sisters, eagerly crowding in at the food bowl. At the moment, he had vanished entirely under the bed, while the others were still cautiously poking their heads in.

"Do they have names?" Ben asked.

Tessa reached under the bed for the small orange kitten. "One of the shelter volunteers called this one Toblerone, because of his color—like the wrapper of a Toblerone bar. She was about nineteen and I think she just liked the sound of the word."

"That's not a bad theme for all of them," Ben suggested. He picked up the other two orange kittens, one in each hand; they instantly commenced purring. "See, these could be Butterfinger and Twix."

"Those are terrible names. Don't you dare."

"There has to be a Kit Kat, of course ..."

Tessa sighed, warming to the game. "This one can be Kit Kat," she suggested, reaching out to stroke the spotted kitten. "What about the other one? There aren't any gray candy bars, thank goodness."

"Milky Way?"

Tessa wrinkled her nose. "I don't like that one."

"Hershey? Snickers?"

"Ugh, they're getting worse. And now I'm hungry. Let's just call her ... Fudge."

"And you didn't like *my* names?" Ben laughed. "As for food, there's chili on the stove. I should probably get back to it before it burns. Sound good?"

"Sounds amazing."

She carefully closed the bedroom door, leaving the kittens to explore their new home, and went with him into the kitchen area at one side of the main living room. Warm, spicy cooking smells filled the cabin.

Ben stirred the pot of chili on the stove with a long wooden spoon. "Don't get your hopes up; it's just chili from a can. I should've stopped at the store on the way up for groceries. There's no milk or bread or anything perishable in the cabin at the moment. But there are crackers to go with it, and a tin of shortbread cookies from last Christmas for dessert."

"It smells wonderful." The small wooden table had been set and, to her delight, a bouquet of fresh wildflowers placed as a centerpiece in a blue glass vase. "Oh, this is lovely; thank you."

"More where that came from," Ben pointed out, ladling chili into two bowls. "And there's great trout fishing in the brook behind the cabin. Tomorrow I'll probably catch us a couple of trout for dinner, but right now I felt like we both needed a quick meal. Have you ever gone fishing?"

Tessa shook her head. "I hope you mean with fishing poles and not ... you know ... paws."

Ben laughed and set her bowl of chili in front of her, followed a moment later by an opened package of Saltine crackers. "You haven't lived until you've crouched on your hands and knees in a mountain stream and caught a trout with your bare fingers."

"I can't tell if you're joking or not."

"Joking," he said with a grin. "Well, to be honest, I *do* go fishing as a panther sometimes. But we'll use poles. There's a nice little pool downstream from the cabin that has good trout fishing on warm afternoons. We could head down there later today, if you like, or just lounge around the cabin."

"I'll see how I feel after I eat." She tried a spoonful of chili, and discovered all in a rush how hungry she was; she hadn't eaten since breakfast early that morning. She inhaled the bowl, hardly waiting for it to cool.

Ben made a pot of coffee, and when they'd finished eating, they took their coffee and the promised tin of cookies into the living room. Ben had opened the windows, and the curtains moved in a light breeze. Outside, the sun was setting over the mountains.

Tessa still couldn't get over how quiet it was here. When she strained her ears, aside from the hum of the refrigerator and an occasional rustle as the kittens explored the bedroom, she couldn't hear a thing. No car horns or traffic or any of the other thousand noises of the city that she'd grown up with. Instinctively she checked her phone, only to find that it had no signal.

"It's so rustic," she said, looking around the cabin as she leaned forward from the couch to set her useless phone on the coffee table; it might as well have been a coaster for all the good it would do her here. "I don't see a TV or a computer, and it's not like you can just run down the street

63

to see a movie or listen to a band playing at your local coffee shop. How do you keep from going out of your mind with boredom?"

"There are plenty of things to do here. That, for example." Ben pointed to the bookshelves lining the walls. "And there's the entire woods to explore, fish to catch, wood to whittle ... But you also have to start thinking differently than you do in town. Time moves more slowly out here. You have to relax and let it happen."

"I'm not very good at relaxing," Tessa admitted.

He set his mug on the coffee table and sat down next to her on the couch. "Here. Let me help."

When his hands first touched her shoulders, she went tense. Ben stayed as he was, one strong hand resting lightly on each shoulder, until her instinctive stiffness at being touched began to ease. Then he increased the pressure slightly, smoothing his hands over her T-shirt-clad shoulders and across the top of her spine.

When his fingertips brushed the skin above the collar of her T-shirt, she tensed again, but for a different reason. Each light touch sent an electric charge through her body, heat quivering down her limbs and melting her at the core.

Ben stroked his thumbs in slow circles over the top of her spine, and leaned forward to kiss the back of her neck. "How's that feeling?"

"I don't know if I'm getting any less tense," she admitted breathlessly. She was all too aware of him behind her, his weight dipping the couch, his legs apart to accommodate her between them.

The gentle circling of his thumbs paused. "Want me to stop?"

"No," she whispered. "Please. Please keep going."

"I hoped you'd say that." There was warm humor in his

voice, and also something else, a charged urgency echoing the heat surging inside her.

He kissed her neck again, as his hands moved down her back, pressing along the line of her spine. She inhaled, then breathed out slowly, as he slid his hands around her sides, until he could cup her breasts in his hands.

"Oh," he murmured against her neck, his breath stirring the short soft hairs and sending another shiver through her. "Oh, I've *wanted* to do that."

Tessa leaned back against him. She wasn't used to the feeling of having someone wrapped around her like this, but it nevertheless felt like coming home. There was something *familiar* about it, the feeling of his lips on her neck and his strong hands lifting the weight of her breasts, thumbs massaging her nipples through her bra and shirt. The way his arms wrapped around her, his thighs spread to accommodate her hips, the solidity of his erection against her ass—it all felt like she was rediscovering something she'd forgotten, the same pieces-slotting-into-place feeling that she'd felt when he kissed her. As if their souls knew each other and had only now found the missing half of themselves.

... all of which was getting harder to concentrate on, as he mouthed her neck and rubbed her peaking nipples. Arousal thrummed in her body. She was hyper-aware of him: the warm masculine scent of his skin, the strength of his arms, the rock-solid wall of his chest.

And she was even more aware of her own reactions, especially the growing need between her legs. She wanted to be touched, and instinctively, she started to reach down to touch herself.

Ben caught her fingers. "That's my job," he murmured against her neck.

She wanted to laugh at his phrasing (*Does that make me the boss? Do you get overtime?*) but then the sensation of his hand sliding down the front of her body made her suck in a breath. He ran his hand over the curve of her stomach and, working his hand under the loose edge of her T-shirt, dipped a finger under the waistband of her jeans. His fingers brushed against her bare skin in a place where no one ever touched. As he worked, one-handed, to unbutton and unzip her jeans, she reached down to help him.

Even though they were both still fully clothed, she was wetter than she could ever remember having been before. Her panties were already soaked through.

With her jeans unzipped, Ben put his hand into her panties. He was still holding her upright, braced against his chest. His fingers brushed over her damp mound and then pressed lightly against it, cupping his hand over her curls.

She moaned softly, arching her body to press herself more firmly into his palm. Her nipples were so hard they ached.

Ben dipped a finger between her folds, into the wet, eager heat.

Her entire body jerked in reaction, and she made a whining sound in the back of her throat. She felt Ben smile against her neck as he slid another finger inside her to join the first. His palm pressed on her mound and the sensitive nub hidden there, applying direct stimulation as his fingers worked at her slippery heat, sliding in and out.

She realized that she'd begun to pant in time with his strokes. Her head was thrown back against his shoulder, eyes closed, and it was only a sudden movement from Ben that jolted her out of a pleasure daze, especially his hand pulling out of her underwear.

"Nnngghh," she protested incoherently, catching him by the wrist. "Don't stop."

"I'm not stopping," he promised. "I want to taste you."

"Oh," she managed as he flipped her over on the couch. By

now she was putty in his hands. He could put her in any position he wanted—at the moment, this was sprawled on the couch with her legs spread apart. Ben pulled her jeans down, followed by her wet panties. He stripped them off and left them on the floor.

There was something unexpectedly erotic about being naked from the waist down, with her top still fully clothed and her socks on. Not that *anything* wouldn't have been erotic at this point. She was so wet that she felt a trickle of moisture on her inner thigh. Ben spread her thighs with his strong hands, and she was already breathing hard in anticipation before his tongue brushed her folds.

Oh. Sparks danced behind her eyelids.

Ben pulled her leg up to give himself better access, spreading her further. She pressed her sock-clad foot against his shoulder and flung her head back against the couch as his warm wet strokes laved her swollen folds.

Heat mounted inside her with astonishing speed. She reached out, groping for him, and he freed a hand from her thigh to lace his fingers through hers, without ever slowing down. The tickle of his other hand moved up her inner thigh and then a finger slipped inside her, pressing on her sensitive inner walls.

It was almost too much. Her entire body seemed to vibrate with a charged energy. She felt her back arch involuntarily, pushing her hips into the couch. Ben responded by speeding up the rhythm of his fingers, his tongue gliding over her clit in fast, fluttering strokes.

"Ben—" she gasped out.

He didn't stop licking to speak, but his fingers tightened on hers, squeezing her hand in wordless reassurance: *I'm here.*

And with that, she tumbled over the edge, delicious electricity coursing through her body in a livewire burst that started with a deep tingling in her hips and arced out to the tips of her fingers and toes.

She surfaced from the tidal wave of pleasure as Ben pulled himself up onto the couch, lifting her so he could hold her in his arms and kiss her with salty lips.

"That was ..." She tried to pull her scattered thoughts together. "Amazing." Taking a deep breath, she opened her eyes to his smiling face and heated gray eyes, dark with arousal. "I think it's your turn now."

"Upstairs," he said. "I'd like to make love to you properly, in a decent bed."

"I'm going to need a minute. My knees still feel like rubber."

Ben grinned. "I have a solution for that."

He untangled himself from her arms, and then, to her shock, scooped her up in his arms, still bare-ass half-naked as she was. He staggered slightly as he got his balance with the extra weight, and Tessa threw her arms around his neck.

"Aren't I too heavy?"

"You could never be," he told her, and with another kiss, started slowly and carefully toward the stairs.

CHAPTER 8

Ben could still taste her salt, making him so hard he ached, but he was determined not to rush things. She'd had an entire lifetime of being ignored, always being put last, never cared for. In all things, but especially in this, he was determined to treat her right.

Tessa steadied them both as he climbed the stairs, one arm around his neck and the other stretching out to trail on the railing. At the top of the stairs she tensed to be let down, but he carried her on into the bedroom, and laid her out on the bed.

She was tousled and glorious, her face still flushed from her earlier orgasm. Her damp, bare caramel thighs, with the dark mound of curls just visible, begged to be parted.

Getting a tight grip on his own libido, Ben knelt beside her on the bed and pulled up her T-shirt. She stretched her arms above her head to strip it the rest of the way off, and arched her back so he could undo her bra. Finally he got his first look at her breasts, tan and gorgeous, with full, dark brown nipples. The crystal on its silver chain nestled between their smooth mounds. They filled his hands, each the perfect size for him to cup in his palm, fingers spread across her soft skin.

Tessa propped herself up on her elbow and reached for the buttons on his shirt. "Unless you've figured out the trick to having sex with clothes on, you're a little overdressed. Or were you going to admire my breasts all day?"

"I could admire your breasts forever."

"That's great," she murmured, undoing his buttons, "but can you admire them without clothes on? Let's spread the eye candy around."

His shed items of clothing went over the edge of the bed, shirt and pants and underwear landing in a crumpled heap, until at last they could meet skin to skin. She was warm to the touch, and if it weren't for the arousal hammering at him, Ben could have stretched out and basked in the touch of her skin for hours. He still wanted to, if she wanted it.

But she was clearly aching for more. Her hips jerked up when he touched her thigh, and she parted her legs eagerly, reaching to guide him in.

Her slick heat enveloped him. The earlier orgasm had left her wet and open, hungry for more. Ben gasped as he sank into her, and he felt her body move responsively under his, her walls tighten around him.

He thrust into her, and she gave a small cry, reaching up to close her arms possessively around him. With each thrust, her hips lifted to meet him and she pulled him down, as if she could draw him even deeper inside. Ben had to clench his teeth, struggling to keep himself from going over the edge. Each of her gasping cries drew him closer to release.

He felt her start to go over, the way her body relaxed under him and then suddenly tensed, and that was what pushed him into his own release, a white-hot wave breaking over him that tore a ragged cry from his throat.

They shuddered through the waves together, and as their

mutual tension relaxed into limp satiation, he sank down beside her and turned his face into the crook of her shoulder.

Inside him, his panther was purring.

~

Ben's shower enclosure was small, but it had good water pressure and plenty of hot water. Tessa's body was still so sensitive that the heat made her shiver, especially when hot water trickled over her nipples and down between her legs.

They'd drowsed together on the bed for awhile, but despite the lassitude of good sex, it was still early enough that she wasn't ready to fall asleep just yet.

She finally stepped out of the shower clean, tired, and languid, more relaxed than she could ever remember being in her life. Ben's towels were enormous and fluffy. She dried off and then realized she hadn't thought to bring anything clean to wear into the bathroom with her.

Well ... that wasn't really a problem, was it?

Ben was on the couch when she came out of the bathroom with the towel draped over her shoulders, reading a book. He looked up, then did a double take and looked up again. "Wow," he whispered, gazing at her in open wonder.

He'd put on a dark T-shirt and jeans, though his feet were still bare and his hair gloriously sex-tousled. She came over the couch and draped an arm over his shoulder, while he tilted his head back to kiss her. It was the casualness of it, more than the physical contact, that took her breath away.

She had a boyfriend. She couldn't get over it.

An incredibly hot, protective boyfriend with a secluded cabin in the mountains.

Could life get any better? Not hardly. Well, maybe if

dragons weren't after her, but hopefully that wouldn't be a problem here.

"Not to be a mood-killer," she murmured, lips brushing his forehead, "but where'd you put my suitcase?"

"Oh, right! I guess you need that, don't you?" He pointed up the stairs. "It's at the top of the stairs. I guess you didn't notice when we went past it earlier."

"I had other things on my mind."

Ben smiled, crinkling his eyes in that way she was coming to love. "Me too."

She was deliciously aware of Ben watching her naked ass as she climbed the stairs and bent over the suitcase.

"You can take it into the bedroom," he called up from downstairs. "I took it up with that in mind, and then thought that you might think I was pushing—you know, putting your clothes in *my* bedroom—so you can take one of the down-stairs bedrooms if you'd rather."

"This is exactly where I want to be," she said over the rail-ing. "So I'll just make myself at home up here, shall I?"

"Please do."

She took the suitcase into the bedroom and opened it on the bed. Old instincts took over, though, and she just got out enough clothes to change into, then closed the suitcase neatly and put it on the floor against the wall. There was a part of her that wanted to unpack and see her clothes nestled against Ben's in the drawers of the big wooden dresser against the wall, but there was an even bigger part that wanted to be ready for a quick getaway.

Would she ever live anywhere without expecting that she was going to have to leave?

She pushed that thought down. With a dragon assassin hunting her, it was a sensible precaution to take. She changed into clean jeans and a black crop-top with MEOW picked out across the breasts in rhinestones (the closest thing to sexy clothes she owned), then almost changed out of it when she looked down at the curve of her exposed belly over the top of her jeans. But, hell, Ben had just seen all of her less than an hour ago.

She padded downstairs, trailing her hand on the railing. Ben looked up and smiled, then smiled wider when he saw what she was wearing. "I like the shirt," he remarked.

"You know, there are people who say women shaped like me shouldn't wear crop-tops."

Ben stood up and came over. He touched the smooth skin of her belly lightly, running his hand over it with obvious delight, then leaned in to kiss her.

"Those people," he murmured against her lips, "are very wrong."

"I'm starting to get that impression."

She was just stretching up to kiss him again when a chorus of high-pitched mewing broke out from the bedroom. Tessa burst into giggles and looked over to see a small orange paw snake out from under the closed bedroom door before vanishing again.

"Oh yes," Ben said, "that. I think the kittens are restless."

"Do you mind if I let them out into the living room? I didn't want to overwhelm them, but it looks like they want to join the family."

"Sure. I'll go close the windows."

When she opened the door, the kitten who had been trying to crawl under it (Toblerone) tumbled into the living room, looked startled, then picked himself up and went to see what was under the couch. The rest fanned out along the edges of the room. One tried to crawl into the fireplace. Tessa caught it and put it on the couch instead.

"Are you supposed to kitten-proof a house, the way you'd child-proof?" Ben asked, watching as the march of the kittens spread to encompass the kitchen and one of them tried to climb the sawhorse. "Because I sort of ... haven't."

"Yes, but it's not as much of a big deal with kittens as it is with toddlers or even puppies." She picked up a cordless drill off the floor under the sawhorse and set it on top. "You want to make sure they can't get into anything toxic, and they might chew on things like electrical cords. Mostly you want to pick up anything they might get tangled in, or anything that could poison them."

They went around the living room checking for hazards and moving appliances out of reach. Ben secured the cabinets under the sink with a loop of twine to stop them from trying to get inside. The kittens were oblivious; the entire world was a fascinating jungle gym, made for kittens to climb on.

"I apologize in advance if they destroy anything."

Ben shrugged. "My friends Derek and Gaby have been up here with their son. He's six. Trust me, I'm not bothered by that sort of thing. Anyway, can I get you anything? Show you where anything is?"

"Let me just look around and see what there is to drink."

"There's still some coffee if you want it. Not much else right now, besides water."

Tessa went into the kitchen, reached for the pot of coffee keeping warm by the stove, then poured herself a glass of water instead. If she started drinking coffee this late at night, she'd never sleep, and she was finally starting to feel like she *could* sleep—relaxed, comfortable, no longer scared or even worried.

Ben was on the couch again, smiling at her. She went over to join him, curling her bare feet under her.

"So what do you *do* in the evening here?" she asked. "Just read?"

"Mostly. I could teach you some card games." He laid his

book aside. "Or we could just talk. There's so much I want to know about you."

"There's nothing interesting about me, though."

"Everything about you is interesting to me," Ben said gently. "Tell me an interesting fact about yourself."

"Uh ... I like cats?"

He laughed. "I already know that one. How about ... hmmm. I don't know anything about you, really. Did you go to college?"

Tessa shook her head, feeling embarrassment creep up her neck in the form of a flush. "No. I couldn't afford it."

Ben picked up her hand and kissed her fingertips lightly. "Did you want to?"

"I don't know. I didn't have anything specific in mind, nothing I wanted to study, I mean." There had been nothing even remotely judgmental in his tone, but talking about herself still made her squirm. "What about you? Did you imagine yourself as a cop when you were a kid?"

"Not really. I've actually got an engineering degree."

Her eyes went wide. "Really?"

"Not what you expected, huh? That was my career for awhile. I traveled all over the world, planning designs for bridges and that sort of thing." He smiled. "Want to hear some stories about that?"

Somehow he recognized that she didn't like talking about herself and was giving her a graceful out. She couldn't get over how he was just ... perfect. "Yes," she said, and she lay down on the couch, snuggling her head into his lap. She could lie here forever, just listening to his voice. "Tell me some stories."

It wasn't even the words so much as his voice. She closed her eyes and drifted as he petted her hair and talked about the places he'd been, the things he'd seen.

He had lived such an interesting life. Why was he interested in *her*? Would he eventually get over his infatuation and leave?

She didn't want to think about that right now. She was comfortable; she felt safe.

She just wanted to stay here forever.

CHAPTER 9

Ben's bed was more than big and comfortable enough for two people to sleep, spooned together. Tessa was awakened in the morning by Ben sitting bolt upright in bed next to her. Early morning sun shafted through the window, turning his skin soft gold and evoking pleasant memories of the night before.

"Mmm?" she managed sleepily.

"I hear an engine. Someone's coming up the driveway."

That cleared the sleep out of her foggy brain. "Your friend Derek, maybe?"

"Maybe." He got out of bed and went to the window, then shook his head and started to dress in a hurry. "But he'd have no reason to think I'm here. I didn't tell him I was coming out to the cabin, and it's not even a weekend. There's no reason why anyone who knows me would visit."

Tessa reached for her clothes as well, spurning the sexy crop-top for another of her oversized T-shirts. "You said no one could follow us here. Is there any way someone could have found us?"

"I don't see how." Ben strapped on his shoulder holster

over a T-shirt. "The cabin's not in my name. Only a handful of people know about it, and I trust all of them. Well, my dad—" He stopped, then shook his head. "No. I *don't* trust my dad, but the exact reasons why I don't trust him are also why I don't think he'd sell us out in a situation like this."

That made exactly zero sense, but Tessa didn't think now was the time to ask him to explain. She could hear the engine now too, a loud coughing roar that sounded like it was coming into the yard of the cabin. "Is that a motorcycle?" she asked.

"Sounds like it," Ben said grimly. "Stay here."

Tessa shook her head. "I'm not letting you face danger without me. Besides, this probably concerns me, and I want to know what's going on."

He huffed a sigh. "Fine, you can come downstairs, but stay out of sight."

Tessa stuffed the pendant down the front of her shirt and bent over to tie her shoes. "I guess there's no chance we could just lock the doors and hope they'll go away."

"With my car outside? I doubt it."

Outside the cabin, the loud, coughing engine died. Ben opened the bedroom door and went down the stairs two at a time, vaulting over a kitten. Tessa followed more quietly, picking up the kitten (it was either Twix or Butterfinger; she couldn't tell them apart) and taking it with her to the bottom of the stairs. If they were going to have to leave, she should start getting them back into their carrier, but for now, she went softly to the window beside the door and peeked out from behind the curtain.

A figure in a black leather jacket was just swinging his leg off a large, gleaming motorcycle, its chrome shining in the morning sun. That was definitely Reive. So much for Ben's assurances that they hadn't been followed.

Ben closed the door behind him and went down the porch steps. "You're a long way from home," he said evenly.

"So are you, panther. So are you." Reive wasn't wearing a helmet, and his black hair was wind-tousled. He pushed a pair of expensive-looking sunglasses to the top of his head.

"This *is* my home. You're trespassing on private property." From her perspective at the window, Tessa saw Ben's arm shift as he moved a hand to the butt of the gun holstered against his side. He hadn't covered it with a jacket this time; the strap cut across the back of his T-shirt in a sharp diagonal slash. "And I'm telling you to leave right now. If you don't, there's going to be trouble."

Reive held his hands out, showing the palms. He didn't appear to have any weapons, though he could be hiding anything under his heavy jacket. "I've told you, my quarrel is not with you. It's the woman you're hiding that I want."

"Leave. Now."

The kitten in Tessa's arms hooked its tiny claws into her shirt. She absently freed its small, soft paw without tearing her eyes away from the window. She knew she shouldn't be delaying like this; she should be packing up the kittens and getting ready to leave. But she couldn't look away from the confrontation in the yard.

"You won't desist, will you?" Reive's words came out resigned.

Ben drew his gun. Tessa had to stifle a gasp. She'd never seen anyone use a gun in real life before. He wasn't pointing it at Reive, but he held it in a way that made it very clear he could raise it in a heartbeat.

"Very well," Reive said. "If it's a fight you want, no one ever accused *me* of bringing a knife to a gunfight."

His last words came out in a rumbling growl ... and he changed.

Tessa recoiled away from the window, the kitten in her

79

arms turning to a snarling, hissing ball of claws. Ben's shift from man to panther had been a gentle transition, his body easing with feline grace from one to the other. This transition was *violent*. Reive erupted in a wall of scales, rearing upward against the clear morning sky. Spikes burst from his neck and shoulders; a pair of wings erupted forth and spread to block the sun. Tessa couldn't even tell what happened to his clothes. They seemed to become part of him, vanishing into his glossy scales.

His lean, spiky body seemed to go up and up forever. The long-jawed reptilian head bowed over Ben like the head of a cobra mesmerizing a mouse. The dragon was copper-colored, gleaming in the sun like a polished brass kettle. A red stripe ran down each side of his body, making it look as if he'd been painted in blood. Each of the claws on his enormous forepaws, poised over Ben like a cat's claws, was as long as a sword.

The kitten wrenched itself from Tessa's arms, leaving bloody scratches down her wrists. The pain recalled her to herself. She had to get the kittens and get out of here. There was no way she could fight something like that. There was no way *Ben* could fight something like that. Their only chance was to flee and find somewhere to hide and ...

... and she didn't know, she didn't know how she was ever going to be free of this, but even running forever was better than being torn apart with those terrible claws.

Base animal instinct told her to just run out the back, to get away as far as possible. But she couldn't leave Ben, and she couldn't abandon the helpless kittens who depended on her.

Right now the nearest of the helpless kittens had wedged itself as far under the couch as it could go. "Come out out," she whispered, afraid to make too much noise for fear the dragon would hear her.

A sudden burst of gunshots outside made her jump with a small scream. The kitten hissed and backed even further under the couch, out of her reach.

"Come on, come on, baby." Tessa fought to keep her voice calm as she strained to reach the kitten in its hiding place. "I'm trying to help you."

The gunshots had to be Ben. A dragon wouldn't carry a gun.

A roar outside the cabin rattled the windows. *That* was the dragon. It was followed by the snap of another gunshot.

With panic breathing down her neck like hot drag-onbreath, Tessa gave up trying to retrieve that particular kitten and went after the other ones. They had all panicked and run for cover, but most of them hadn't been as successful at finding a hiding place. She scooped up one of them in a corner of the kitchen and caught another under a chair.

A tremendous crash shook the cabin and sent adrenaline jolting through her, almost making her drop the kittens. *I have to get out of here!* She sent her desperately worried good wishes in Ben's direction as she took the kittens into the back bedroom.

Here she discovered another problem.

The kittens hadn't objected to being stuffed into the carrier at the shelter. It was a new experience for them, so all she'd had to do was grab them and pop them in, one by one. This time, however, they knew what was coming, and they did not like it at all.

It was amazing how one small kitten could suddenly consist of about ten legs and 400 claws, half of them attempting to hold off the carrier and the other half aimed at Tessa's hand and arm.

"Get in there!" Tessa ordered between her teeth, jamming Kit Kat down just as Toblerone tried to make a break for it. "I could just abandon you ungrateful little jerks, you know!"

Sobbing with frustration and fear, she managed to get them all jammed inside and zipped up, along with another she found cowering under the bed. She was tempted to just leave the other two (one under the sofa, the other hiding in some unknown location), but what if the dragon burned down the cabin? Could real dragons breathe fire?

And once she caught the kittens, what then? She and Ben were going to have to escape past *that* thing.

If Ben was even still alive. She hadn't heard any gunshots lately. Panic choked her, not for herself, but for the man who, in so short a time, had become so much a part of her that she couldn't imagine her life without him.

～

Ben stood his ground as the dragon reared above him. Even if he was willing to consider running—and there wasn't a chance, not with Tessa in the cabin— it wouldn't do him much good. The dragon wasn't really built for sprinting, but with those wings, it could follow him anywhere.

He'd watched his father shift on more than one occasion, so this wasn't the first time he'd seen a dragon in the flesh. It still never got easy. They were not just huge, but alien-looking, every part of their body adapted to be the most powerful and efficient predator in the modern world ... perhaps the most effective predator the world had ever seen.

The sudden, incongruous image of a dragon fighting a dinosaur popped into Ben's head. His lips twitched.

"Why are you smiling?" Reive demanded, his voice a deep rumble. Dragons were among the only shifters who could speak in their animal form.

"Just wondering if you'd win in a fight against a T-rex."

Reive stared down at him. "Are you stalling?"

"Not really. Just giving you a chance to change your mind. If you don't shift back immediately, I won't hesitate to use lethal force against you."

He wasn't sure if the curl of Reive's lip was amusement or contempt. "Puny little shifter, you couldn't hurt me if you tried."

Ben squeezed off a fusillade of bullets at him.

Despite his warning, he was trying to stop Reive, not kill him, so rather than aiming for the head, he fired into center mass: in this case, Reive's chest, a broad expanse of shimmering copper scales. That would've been a kill shot on a human, but given Reive's size, Ben wasn't even sure if the .38 would have enough stopping power to penetrate his scales.

Reive grunted, more in surprise than pain. Bright blood glistened on his chest, so at least the bullets had done some damage, but he showed no signs of being badly hurt.

"Really?" Reive rumbled. "You think that's going to stop me?"

"Worth a try." Maybe he should've gone for a headshot after all. By his count, he had four shots left—and no spare ammo, because it was all in his jacket (still in the house) and in his car.

Not that reloading would help a whole lot, unless what he was reloading was a cannon.

Reive had been crouching on his back legs, making himself nearly as tall as the roof of the cabin; now he crashed down to all fours, his massive foreclaws tearing chunks out of the meadow turf. His body was low-slung, the shoulders angled slightly outward like an alligator's.

"Listen," he said, staring at Ben down his long scaled snout. "This isn't your fight. I have no quarrel with you. I just need the girl."

"You're going to kill her."

"Well, yes, obviously, but that doesn't have to be *your* problem."

"Even leaving aside the fact that I'm a cop, and I'm not just going to let you *eat* someone—"

"Eurgh, I'm not going to eat her! What kind of barbarian do you think I am?"

"—every one of her problems is my problem too," Ben said. "She's my mate."

It was hard to read expression on Reive's inhuman features, but a frisson of some sharp emotion passed across his face. "No wonder you're so persistent. Suppose I can't expect you to get out of the way, then."

"Nope," Ben said, and shot him in the face.

He aimed for the eye, one of the few parts of Reive's well-armored dragon body where he thought the gun's tiny bullets could do serious damage, but Reive's reflexes were hideously fast, faster even than those of most shifters. The dragon jerked his head to the side. Blood sprayed anyway, and for a moment Ben couldn't tell if he'd actually managed to put an eye out, but then Reive opened his eyes, the right slightly bloodshot with a mask of blood around it. The bullet must have grazed the lid or winged the softer, less scaled flesh just beneath it.

"Honorless scoundrel," Reive growled, and lashed out with one huge forepaw.

Dragons were fast, but panthers were fast, too. Ben sprang out of the way, keeping a firm grip on his gun. He would've vastly preferred a larger weapon (a bazooka might have come in handy) but at least the pistol didn't interfere with his ability to maneuver.

If he survived this, maybe it would be a good idea to invest in a hunting rifle to keep in the cabin. He didn't own one because, when he hunted, it wasn't on two legs.

However, a larger weapon than his service sidearm might come in handy in case of—

—unexpected dragon attacks? Okay, so this wasn't the kind of situation likely to come up again. Hopefully.

"Hold still," Reive snarled, swiping at him again. Ben ducked behind one of the rough-hewn wooden poles supporting the porch roof; it splintered under the blow driven by Reive's powerful shoulder muscles.

"So you can claw me to death? I don't think so!"

He wanted to draw Reive away from the cabin, but didn't dare try. Reive wasn't stupid. The dragon had to guess Tessa was in there.

Would she have the presence of mind to try to escape while Ben held off Reive? So far, she hadn't come out or made a sound that he could hear. The cabin had no back door, but the windows in the bedrooms were large enough to get in and out of. Derek had told Ben that he'd gone in through a window while his mate's family was being held hostage in the cabin last year.

Ben wished true telepathy went along with the mate bond. Longtime mated pairs joked about being able to read each other's minds, but so did long-married human couples. It was really just a matter of being completely in sync with each other, and reading the other's small tells.

Still, he thought desperately at Tessa, *Get out! Don't worry about me!*

"This is such a waste of time," Reive complained, shaking splinters out of his claw. The porch roof sagged alarmingly over Ben's head.

"If your time is that precious to you, I have a suggestion. Leave."

"I would if I could." Reive reared on his back legs and smacked a paw on the unstable end of the porch roof. Ben dodged out of the way as it crashed down where he'd been standing.

And I just got done fixing the cabin from the damage last summer!

"But I can't return to my clan empty-handed," the dragon went on, weaving his head in an attempt to locate Ben in the rubble. "I've been given a task and I'm honor-bound to complete it."

"What'd she *do*, anyway? She doesn't even know what dragons *are!*"

"Not my problem," Reive growled, stalking toward him. The tip of his tail, just visible in the long grass, twitched like a cat's.

"Oh really? What about honor? Is it honorable to kill an enemy who has no idea what you want from them, without even giving them a chance to explain or offer an alternative?"

"You know," Reive said, "killing *her* is a necessary and unpleasant duty, but I'm starting to rather look forward to killing *you*."

Good, Ben thought. *Chase me, not her.*

Inside his chest, his panther snarled. *Let me at him!*

The urge to shift was strong, but as a panther, he'd lose his human advantages: the gun, the opposable thumbs. Still, it wasn't like either of those was doing him any good at the moment. And he would have his panther's weapons, the sharp teeth and claws that his human body lacked.

"Enough stalling," Reive growled, and swung a paw at him. Ben dodged, but Reive clipped his arm, knocking him to the ground. The gun fell from his numb fingers.

Let me fight! His panther was nearly frantic. *We're going to die—and our mate will too!*

The panther was right. He couldn't win like this; he didn't even have a chance. Ben didn't bother taking his clothes off this time. With the dragon poised to spring, there was no time.

He felt his panther take over, his human clothes parting along the seams as the cat leaped out of him. A shrug of his shoulder sent his holster falling into the grass, and then the lean black panther sprang out of the way of the dragon's next scimitar-clawed swipe.

"Oh, you do have some fight in you, then. I wondered what kind of shifter you were." The dragon shrugged and turned back toward the cabin. "Not that it matters. You can't stop me."

Ben sank his teeth into the dragon's tail. Reive hissed and whipped his head around, but Ben was already gone into the grass. Still, the dragon was horribly fast. One clawed forepaw crashed to the ground inches from Ben's whiskered nose; the next blow caught him in a vicious slap and sent him tumbling end over end.

As Ben struggled to get to his feet, dazed and reeling, blinking blood out of his eyes, he saw the dragon lunge up the cabin's porch and knock the door off its hinges with a casual slap of a paw.

When the dragon crashed through the door, Tessa—dusty and scratched—was halfway under the couch, her fingers brushing against kitten fur.

Tessa screamed, letting the end of the couch crash back to the floor as she recoiled in shock. The kitten zipped out from under the other end of the couch and shot across the floor to cower beneath a chair.

"Trying to hide won't save you," the dragon growled.

"I'm trying to rescue my kittens, you beast," Tessa yelled,

so terrified that she barely heard the words coming out of her mouth. "Where's Ben?"

"Don't worry about him. You're the one in trouble."

The dragon thrust his massive head through the door. Tessa screamed again, snatched up the squalling kitten carrier, and ran into the kitchen. The dragon's shoulders, too wide to fit, crunched against the doorframe as he tried to push his way through.

Looking around wildly for a weapon, Tessa spotted a large cast-iron frying pan hanging behind the stove. She grabbed it with her free hand and started beating him in the snout with wild swings.

"I have to say I admire your fighting spirit," the dragon remarked. He winced and turned his head to catch her makeshift cast-iron club on the armored side of his jaw rather than the sensitive snout-tip. "It gives me no pleasure to do what I must do."

"It gives me even less pleasure, believe me!" She punctuated her words by slamming the pan repeatedly into his face. "Where! Is! Ben! You! Monster!"

"Aargh! Stop that." The dragon wrestled one of his legs inside the cabin; the doorframe crunched and buckled. "It'd be easier and less painful for you if you'd cooper—"

Tessa whacked him in the teeth. With irritation that could be read even on his reptilian face, the dragon snapped his teeth shut on her makeshift weapon. Tessa engaged in a very brief tug-of-war that the dragon won, wrenching the pan out of her hands. He spat it out with a clang.

Tessa grabbed a canister of black pepper, opened it with her teeth, and flung it at his face.

"Troublesome little—*atchoo!*"

While the dragon coughed and sneezed, a terrified orange blur sped past Tessa's feet. She bent down, grabbed the kitten, and performed the hastiest kitten-stuffing maneuver of her life on the kitchen counter, jamming him on top of the others and holding them down while she zipped the carrier shut again.

If there was an Olympic gold medal for kitten-wrangling, she felt like she'd earned it.

The dragon blinked watering eyes at her and, with another heave of his shoulders, broke out more of the doorframe and got his other leg inside, scraping off a shower of copper scales. Now half of him was in the living room and he could easily reach her.

Tessa backed up into a corner of the kitchen. She was trapped, but she wasn't going down without a fight. She seized one canister after another, pelting him with sugar and salt, raisins and a shower of nuts.

"Really?" the dragon said. As Tessa ran out of projectiles, he opened his jaws.

One of the living room windows imploded as Ben's black panther came crashing through in a cascade of shattered glass and curtains.

He launched himself at the dragon's head, swiping a paw across its face. Reive roared as Ben's claws slashed across one of his eyes.

Ben hit the ground and shifted human in an instant. His face and shoulder were bloody; Tessa gasped in shock. "Out the window!" he ordered. "My car keys are with my clothes. Get—" He broke off and rolled out of the way as the dragon snapped at him.

"There's still one kitten in here, and I don't know where it is!"

"Forget it! Just go!"

Easier said than done, Tessa thought, eyeing the window. To get to it, she had to get past the dragon.

Seeing her predicament, Ben offered her an opening by backing up against the far wall of the living room, trapping himself but leaving her a clear path to the window. He shifted again, dropping on all fours to the floor, and sank his teeth into the dragon's leg.

Tessa screwed up her courage and dashed across the room. She dropped the kitten carrier out of the window, and wriggled out after it, falling into the long grass beside the cabin.

After the chaos inside, it seemed incredibly peaceful and serene out here, except for an occasional thump from behind the cabin wall. Tessa gulped down a couple breaths of the meadow-scented air, and then picked up the cat carrier and ran around to the front of the cabin.

It looked like there had been a heck of a fight here. The ground was churned up, the grass flattened, and one side of the porch roof had caved in. The dragon's coppery hindquarters—all of him that was visible, with the rest inside the cabin—shifted this way and that as he tried to attack Ben.

Tessa's first thought was that finding Ben's clothes out here was going to be like hunting for a needle in a haystack, but then she saw the glint of his gun, and found a pile of torn-up clothing next to it. *So that's what happens when he shifts in his clothes.* She retrieved his keys and, while she was at it, scooped up his gun and his phone, stuffing them hastily into a side pocket on the cat carrier. Then she ran to the car, threw the carrier in the back, and half-fell into the driver's seat.

The car started easily, and Tessa took a deep breath for what felt like the first time since Reive had shown up at their door. She was in a car with the engine running. She could *get away*.

Except ... Ben was still in the cabin.

She had Ben's gun, but she didn't know how to use it, and she was afraid to try. What if she missed the dragon and hit Ben instead?

Instead, she revved the engine and rammed Ben's car into the dragon's hindquarters.

It felt like hitting a brick wall. The dragon's back legs went out from under him, and there was a startled roar from inside the cabin. A moment later the dragon began to writhe, trying to back out, and Tessa realized he was stuck in the doorway.

Ben's panther leaped out the shattered window. He landed awkwardly, stumbling; he was clearly hurt.

And he had a kitten in his mouth, carrying it by the scruff of the neck like a momma cat.

Shifting human again, he dropped the confused-looking kitten into his hand and tumbled into the car through the passenger-side door, cradling the kitten against his bare chest.

"Are you—" She started to ask if he was all right, but he was covered in blood and dirt; clearly he wasn't.

The dragon thrashed as he tried to get out of the cabin doorway.

"His motorcycle," Ben panted. He leaned into the backseat to put the kitten in the carrier with the others. "Ram his motorcycle. Push it into the creek behind the cabin."

"What? Why?"

"Just do it!"

It seemed like a ridiculous waste of time. The dragon didn't need the motorcycle to pursue them; it had wings! But Tessa trusted Ben. She gunned the motor and the car thumped into the motorcycle. The wheels started to spin. Tessa accelerated, and the motorcycle was pushed backward, tearing a swath through the meadow grass.

"Push it where?"

"Creek! Behind the cabin!"

She gunned the engine and the car sped up. Ben suddenly shouted, "Stop!" and Tessa slammed on the brakes. The motorcycle tumbled over a small embankment and there was a tremendous splash.

"Now go, go! Get out of here!"

Tessa didn't need the urging. She whipped the car around, accelerated past the still-trapped (but rapidly escaping) dragon, and jolted onto Ben's overgrown driveway.

"Why did you have me do that?" she asked as the car bounded over ruts, branches whipping across the windshield. She had to cling to the steering wheel with both hands. Losing control at this speed would probably mean slamming into a tree and killing them both. In the backseat, the distressed kittens wailed.

"It's part of his hoard," Ben said.

"*What?*"

"Dragons prize their hoards above all else." Ben twisted around, trying to see out of the car's rear window. "Damage a dragon's belongings and you might as well hurt them directly. If it's a choice between chasing us or getting the motorcycle out of the creek before it's too damaged to salvage, he'll go for the motorcycle first."

Tessa was not at all convinced, but they didn't seem to have an angry dragon chasing them yet, so she would just have to believe him. She fishtailed out onto the main road. "Which way?"

"There's really only one way." Ben pointed. "Toward town. The other way, the road just goes up into the mountains and dead-ends. We'd be trapped."

"I feel trapped anyway!" She pushed down the accelerator, picking up speed, all too aware of how easy they would be to spot from the air. "We're sitting ducks out here."

"I know. We have to get to the main highway. Once we get there, he'll have to guess our direction randomly. And there'll be more witnesses in other vehicles."

"Why does that matter?"

"Dragons don't want to be discovered," Ben said. "He'll be less likely to chase us if he might be seen."

Right now, they were alone on the rural road; they hadn't passed a single other car. At least she didn't have to worry about dodging other traffic. Navigating the curves at this speed was bad enough.

"How long do you think he'll wait before—" She shut up as a shadow fell over the car. "Oh shit."

"My sentiments exactly," Ben said grimly. He rolled down his window a crack to look out.

"Damn, damn, damn," Tessa whimpered. She pressed down the accelerator, pushing the car up past 60 despite the sharply winding road. "What's he doing?"

"I think he's having trouble keeping up. Don't slow down."

She glimpsed the dragon in the rearview mirror, a flash of his broad-winged shape against the blue sky as they whipped around a turn. Then Ben's head blocked her view as he craned into the backseat.

"Ben, sit still! I can't see!"

"New problem," Ben said. "Your kittens are getting out."

"Are you *kidding* me!"

Tessa risked a glance over her shoulder to see that the frantic kittens had torn open a gap in the soft-sided carrier. Two of them were already loose in the backseat, tumbling over each other as they crawled around, exploring. Another one was in the process of squeezing its way out of the hole.

"Get your gun!" she said. "It's back there with the carrier. They might, I don't know, accidentally shoot us or something."

"The kittens have my gun," Ben muttered. "This is the worst day ever." He struggled up to his knees in the seat, gasping in pain. Tessa tried not to let herself be distracted by his bare hip and pale flank as he leaned into the backseat.

She had more than enough distractions already. One of

the orange kittens squirmed quickly through the gap between the seats and plunked into her lap. There were mewls and the sound of claws on upholstery all over the backseat. Every last one of the little jerks was loose back there now, from the sound of things.

I am suing whoever made that carrier! Tessa thought desperately. *Kittenproof, my ass!*

Wind whipped suddenly into the car, ruffling her hair. "Did you roll down your window again?" Tessa cried, trying to keep her eyes on the road as the kitten in her lap batted at the steering wheel. She caught another glimpse of the dragon flashing overhead; he was making up time since she'd slowed down because of the kittens. "Roll it back up! They'll fall out!"

"It wasn't me," Ben said, with a grunt of pain; he was draped over his seat now, half of him in the backseat. "They're trying to climb the doors; I think one of them got a foot on the window controls."

Tessa took another startled glance over her shoulder. To her horror, she saw that the driver-side back window was halfway down, with one of the kittens actually trying to climb up to reach it. "Are you telling me the *kittens* rolled down the window?!"

"Yes." Ben stretched across the backseat, trying to reach the window controls. "Where did you say you put my gun?"

"It's in a pocket of the—"

"Watch the turn!"

Tessa hastily looked forward, yelped in dismay, and slammed on the brakes, cranking the steering wheel through a tight turn an instant before they went off the road into the woods. There was a series of thumps from the backseat as various items, including kittens, tumbled into the rear footwell. The kitten on Tessa's lap tumbled across her knees and fell on her feet.

Her feet ... which were currently driving the car.

"No!" she said, trying to keep her right foot on the gas while using her left foot to fend off the kitten. "No, get out of there! Bad kitten! Ben! Help!"

"Kinda busy right now!"

"Me too!" Tessa wailed.

The car was on a straight stretch, so she risked bending down and groping under her feet until she got a hand on the kitten and was able to fling it (gently as possible) out of the footwell in the general direction of the passenger seat. Ben grabbed for it, missed, and made a startled noise as the kitten scrabbled up his bare back and jumped onto the dashboard.

"Get off there!" Tessa freed a hand from the steering wheel to swipe at the kitten, trying to get it out of her field of vision.

The kitten's foot slipped down onto the radio controls. Suddenly AC/DC blared deafeningly into the car.

I definitely feel like I'm *on a highway to hell,* Tessa thought grimly. She got a hand on the kitten, plucked it off the dashboard, and tossed it over Ben's head into the backseat.

Ben shouted something.

"What?" Tessa yelled over the blaring electric guitars. She slapped wildly at the radio, trying to turn it off. It didn't help that she was driving an unfamiliar car and had no idea where the controls for anything were.

"I said I can't see the dragon anymore!"

"Is that good?"

She got her answer an instant later when she whipped around another turn and something huge blocked the road in front of her. Tessa shrieked and stomped on the brake pedal. The car fishtailed wildly, kittens and other loose items went tumbling across the backseat, and Ben's naked body squashed her against the window. Somehow she managed to keep hold of the steering wheel and stopped them about ten feet from the dragon standing in the middle of the road, head up and wings raised, one eye half-closed with bloody claw marks around it. If dragons could look annoyed, this one definitely did.

"I think he's pissed about the motorcycle," Tessa murmured. "Um, not that this isn't nice, but—"

"Yeah. Sorry." Ben struggled off her, back into his own seat. As he did so, a kitten plopped into her lap. She caught it reflexively and tossed it to Ben, who tossed it hot-potato-style into the backseat and then bent down to reach into the footwell in front of his seat.

"What are you doing?" Tessa hissed. The dragon hadn't made a move in their direction yet. She had a feeling Reive was still figuring out what to do. Or possibly just deciding between the many different possible ways to kill them.

"Gun," Ben said. He sat up with it, grimacing in pain. Holding the gun in his bare lap, he popped out the magazine and then slapped it back in.

"How many bullets do you have?"

"Three."

Tessa couldn't tear her eyes away from the enormous predator in the road. "That doesn't seem like enough to me."

Ben let out a short, choked laugh. "Yeah, this caliber isn't too effective on something that size either, so it might not matter how many we have."

"You mean he's *bulletproof*?"

"Not entirely, but it'd have to be a one-in-a-million shot."

"Maybe I can drive around him," Tessa suggested.

Ben shook his head. "All he has to do is stomp on the car and he'd crush it flat, and us along with it." He took a deep breath. "Okay, here's what we're going to do. I'll get out and distract him—"

"I hate this plan already. No splitting up."

"If I can give you a chance to escape—"

"No!" Tessa said. "Look, it's me he's after, right? If anyone should distract him so the other can get away, it ought to be me."

Ben gave her a horrified look. "I'm not going to run off and leave you."

"Right, so don't expect me to do the same thing."

He huffed a soft laugh and gave her a small smile. "Fine, I get it. We're in this together."

"Exactly." Tessa removed a kitten from the steering wheel and tossed it into the backseat. "Any plans that *don't* involve heroic sacrifices?"

"I hate to say it, but I think shooting him in the face and driving as fast as we can looks like our best bet." He turned as the dragon took a step forward. "And I guess we better do it quick, while we still have a choice."

"Ready," Tessa said. She shifted the car into gear, foot pressed down on the brake, and blocked another kitten with her elbow.

Ben was just reaching for the controls to roll down the window when a silver streak dived out of the sky, seemingly out of nowhere, and slammed into the dragon.

Reive staggered off the road, knocking over a few small trees. As the silver creature stumbled to a stop, narrowly missing the car, Tessa realized it was another dragon. This one was much smaller and more slender than the huge copper dragon, though "small" by dragon standards was still larger than the car.

"Is that one on our side?" Tessa asked, her hands white-knuckled on the steering wheel.

"Yes," Ben said. He was grinning. "Oh, yes."

Reive picked himself up, growling, and Ben stopped smiling. The silver dragon was clearly outmatched. As Reive stalked toward the smaller dragon, Tessa couldn't help thinking of a small dog picking a fight with a larger one.

The silver dragon curled its head over its shoulder, neck

bending in a graceful loop. "Go!" it shouted. Its voice was higher-pitched than the other dragon's, and beautifully musical, like the harmonies of a pipe organ.

Tessa didn't need to be told twice; she slammed her foot on the accelerator. Reive started to spread his wings to pursue them, but the silver dragon lunged at him, dragging him back to earth with gleaming steel-colored claws.

Ben kept staring back as they tore off down the road. Slowly he lowered his gun, and absently caught a kitten trying to crawl into the front seat.

"Do you know that other dragon?" Tessa asked—words she never thought she'd hear come out of her mouth.

"Yeah," Ben said softly. He plucked a stray kitten off the back of her seat. "You do, too."

"I don't know any dragons!"

"You do," Ben said. "Melody."

"Wait, *what*? Melody's a *dragon*?"

"Didn't you recognize her voice?"

"No!" Tessa said, but even as she said it, she realized that there *had* been a familiar cadence to the dragon's pipe-organ tones.

"I can't believe she did that." Ben was looking back again. "Dragons aren't allowed to interfere in other dragons' business—not like that. They might cast her out, or worse."

"What? She saved our lives!"

"There's no room for sympathy or mercy in dragons' honor," Ben said. "Or for family either." He sounded sad.

Tessa glanced back. The site of the battling dragons was hidden by twists of the road; all she could see were trees. "From what I can see, it looks like Melody chose family over honor today."

CHAPTER 10

They stopped very briefly just outside Autumn Grove to resolve their urgent kitten issue. Ben—after glancing around for witnesses—jumped out of the car, naked, and opened the trunk. "Here," he said, popping the lid off a Rubbermaid tote. It was full of winter gear and emergency supplies, which Ben dumped unceremoniously into the bottom of the trunk. "This ought to hold them."

"Do you have anything to make air holes?"

Ben got a screwdriver out of his toolbox. He took over driving, while Tessa sat in the backseat with the tote full of kittens and punched holes in the lid.

"Where are we going?" she asked. They'd passed through downtown Autumn Grove and turned onto the highway.

"We need to find a motel, preferably one off the road. As soon as we find somewhere to stop, I'll call my friend Derek and have him bring us some clothes."

"How bad are you hurt? Are you okay to drive?"

"I'm handling it," was all he said.

After the better part of a very tense hour, with both of

them frequently checking the rear-view mirror, Ben turned off suddenly into a small town beside the highway. He drove around the tiny downtown until Tessa pointed out a motel.

"You're going to have to pay for it, I'm afraid," he admitted. "Unless you also grabbed my wallet when you got the gun."

"I didn't get your wallet, but I did get your phone. It's in the carrier, too."

Ben perked up a little, though he still looked weak and pale, as well as filthy and bloody. Tessa left him in the car, calling his friend Derek, while she went into the motel to arrange for a room.

The motel was a tiny family establishment that allowed her to pay with cash, to her surprise; she hadn't even known places like that existed anymore, though it took nearly all her cash. She gave their names as Bob and Tina Gunderson, and requested a room around at the back, "for privacy."

The entire time, she was very aware of the clerk nervously studying her scruffed-up hair, cat-scratched arms, and stained T-shirt. She'd rolled out of bed without so much as touching a brush to her hair, got chased by a dragon, and had a bloody naked man draped on her, and she was pretty sure all of it showed.

"Family vacations, huh?" she said with a weak attempt at a smile, hoping they didn't have a good enough view through the window of the motel to notice that the driver of the car was stark naked and covered in blood.

"Do you have pets with you?" the clerk asked, taking another look at her arms.

"A cat," she said. "A small cat. Very well-behaved. Small pets are okay, right?"

She ended up shoving another twenty across the counter as a pet deposit. That left just enough cash to buy a couple gallons of gas or dinner at McDonald's without having to dip into her credit cards, which were mostly maxed out and would leave a trail anyway.

What are we going to do? she wondered as she went back out to the car with the motel key. She'd had to leave all her spare clothes and even the cat food behind. They had nothing except the clothes on their backs ... and Ben didn't even have that much.

Oh, and five hyperactive kittens.

"Derek's on the way," Ben said, sliding over so she could get in the driver's seat and move the car to park outside their room. "He'll be here in an hour or so with the stuff we need."

"I hope that includes money, because I used just about the last of it getting this room."

"I'm sorry about—"

"Ben, stop apologizing. You remember I'm the reason why we're both in this mess in the first place, right? You could've just walked away and left me at the shelter."

His pain-tense face relaxed into a smile. "No, I couldn't have."

She had to help him out of the car. He leaned on her heavily as she unlocked their room door. "Are you sure I shouldn't be taking you to a hospital instead of a motel in the middle of nowhere?"

Ben shook his head with a pained grimace. "Shifters heal fast. I'll be fine. All I really need is sleep and food. I can get the first here, and Derek's bringing the second."

Tessa's stomach growled, reminding her that they'd been rousted out of the cabin without having a chance to stop for breakfast. "Lunch sounds great. What's he bringing, do you know?"

"I don't know. I just said 'food, and a lot of it'."

She helped him sit down on the bed, and went back for the kittens—keeping them in the tote-carrier for now—before locking the door and making sure the blinds were closed. The room was small and musty, with a pervasive smell of stale cigarette smoke despite the NO SMOKING sign on the door. The carpet was threadbare; the one bed barely looked big enough to accommodate two people.

But it was clean, and the bathroom had decent water pressure and very hot water. She washed her face and hands, then soaked a washcloth and picked up a towel. Ben was lying down when she came out of the bathroom, looking like he'd simply flopped down where he was sitting; he hadn't even bothered to pull a blanket over himself.

"Let me help you get some of that off. Unless you think you could manage a shower."

Ben cracked his eyes open. "Actually, a shower sounds pretty good."

"Do you ... want help?"

His faint smile warmed his gray eyes. "That'd be nice."

At least there were no clothes to try to get off him without hurting him. She shed her clothes on the bathroom floor and cranked the water all the way. Under the hot spray, she gently washed Ben with the cheap mini-bottle of shampoo from the back of the sink.

Despite the amount of blood, he wasn't hurt as badly as she'd feared. The dragon's claws had scored his shoulder and chest, and he was bruised from getting knocked around, as well as having hit his head hard enough to break the skin open and soak his dark hair with blood. But it was mostly superficial, and the gashes had already closed up. She tried to wash them gently so as not to start them bleeding again. Pinkish water swirled down the drain.

"Hold still," she murmured, working the last of the soap into his hair.

"Mmmm." If he was a cat, he'd be purring. He melted into her, and leaned against the side of the shower enclosure as she washed him thoroughly and followed it up with a kiss on his lips, wet from the shower spray.

Ben dragged her lip lightly through his bottom teeth, then pulled away and smiled at her through the shower's haze. "You're still the most gorgeous thing I've ever seen, but don't get your hopes up too much. I don't know how much activity I have in me right now, after everything this morning."

"And you're the most gorgeous thing I've seen," she said, looping an arm carefully around him to turn off the shower. "I would love nothing more than to have you lay me gently down in bed and have your way with me, but right now I'm going to lay *you* gently down in bed so you can get some sleep."

"There's also the likelihood that Derek will interrupt us any minute," Ben said as she gently patted him dry with a scratchy motel towel.

"Yes, that too."

She didn't voice aloud the possibility of a different kind of interruption. But she noticed that when they got out of the shower, Ben took his gun from where she'd placed it on top of the cat tote, checked the remaining bullets, and put it under his pillow before crawling into bed.

Kittenish squalling and claw-scrabbling started up inside the tote. "Would it bother you if I let the kittens out?" Tessa asked. "I hate keeping them cooped up in there."

"Sure," Ben mumbled. "Go ahead."

Tessa popped the lid off, and the muffled chorus of distressed mewing escalated suddenly to full volume. She had put the carrier inside the tote so they had a soft place to curl up, but from the look of things, all they'd done was climb on it and flatten it. Small furry faces turned up to her and little sharp-toothed mouths opened in anxious mewls.

"Hi, little guys. It's okay." She lifted them out one by one. The most anxious ones instantly vanished under the bed, but the rest of them set off to explore, creeping cautiously around the baseboards and trying to climb the dangling bedcovers.

Tessa noticed that they'd used one corner of the tote as a litterbox, which reminded her that she'd had to leave behind all the kitten supplies. "Ben, I don't suppose your friend Derek would mind picking up some kitten food, too?"

Ben plucked a kitten off his face, sighed, and sat up. "May as well. I can talk to him when he gets here."

"I'm sorry," Tessa said contritely, retrieving the one from the bed, only to see another appear over the opposite side. "I was afraid they'd bother you."

"I don't think I'd sleep anyway. I'm too tense." He rubbed a hand across his face, and adjusted the pillows to prop himself against the head of the bed. The newly arrived kitten crawled into his lap. Tessa could hear it purring from where she was sitting on the floor beside the bed.

"We need a plan," she said, picking tiny kitten claws out of her shirt so she could set down the one she was holding. Not to be deterred, it started climbing her leg. "How do we stop this guy from coming after us?"

"I ... can think of some people I could talk to about that," Ben said, his gaze distant.

"Melody?"

"Among others."

"You know more dragons, then." It wasn't a question. "Well, I guess you must. Because of Melody. But ... she's your sister." She had been trying not to think too much about that part, but it kept popping back up, like something submerged that kept floating to the surface. "Ben, *you* aren't a dragon, are you?"

"You've seen me shift," Ben pointed out.

"Yes, but I don't know anything about how dragons work.

For all I know, maybe it's possible for someone to be a dragon and a panther at the same time."

"It's not," Ben said quietly. "Believe me, I'd know. And anyway ... I wouldn't lie to you."

"I know," she said, feeling stabbed. "I didn't mean to imply that I thought you were. So how did Melody come to be, then? Is she adopted?" This sent another stab through her chest. All these years, when she'd envied Melody her happy family—what if they'd had that in common all along, and Melody had never told her? "Or ... are *you* adopted?"

"No, she's not, and I'm not. We're half siblings. Same father, different mothers."

"Ohhhh," Tessa said. "So Melody's mother is a dragon."

"Both her parents are dragons. I'm the odd one out. My mother is a panther shifter."

"Your father is a *dragon?*"

Ben nodded. He looked slightly embarrassed.

"That must be ..." She hesitated. "Actually, I have no idea what that would be like. None at all. What *is* that like?"

"It's normal for me," Ben pointed out. "I grew up with it, so it was just regular life. Like anyone growing up with two divorced parents. My mom didn't have a whole lot to do with my dad, and my dad didn't want a whole lot to do with me, since I'm not a dragon."

Ben's earlier words about dragons came back hauntingly. *Dragon families are very close-knit. Not very welcoming of anyone they don't consider part of the clan.* He'd been speaking from experience. "You and your dad don't get along?"

Ben shook his head. "Not really. I think he's been making a little more of an effort lately, but he still never lets me forget what a disappointment I am."

"Could he help us against Reive?"

"No," Ben said flatly.

"Melody did."

"I know, and she's going to be in awful trouble with Dad because of it. Everything I've told you about draconic honor is stuff Dad taught me. He really takes it seriously, and he tried to impress on us to take it seriously too."

"Yes, but this is life and death! All that is fine, but surely if your life is literally in danger, he'll change his mind—"

"He won't," Ben said simply. "A dragon like my dad won't interfere in another dragon's business. He'd let me die rather than break his code of honor."

Tessa looked up at him. There was no denying the flat certainty in his gaze ... or the veiled pain. All her life, she had wished she'd been able to know her parents, but if this was what having parents was like, suddenly she wondered if she might not be better off as she was.

Especially if her parents had done something so terrible that someone had sent dragons after her because of it ...

A sharp knock at the door made her jump. Tessa opened her mouth, but Ben raised a hand. He got quietly out of bed, retrieved his gun from under the pillow, and went to the door as the knock came again. It was followed an instant later by a male voice. "Keegan, if you're in there, I've got your shit."

"Derek," Ben said on a sigh, and unlocked the door.

Tessa's first impression, especially sitting on the floor, was: *Wow, he's HUGE.* Ben wasn't a small guy, but Derek was much taller and broader—not a speck of fat on him, just solid muscle, his wide shoulders straining at the T-shirt he wore with a truck-stop logo on it. His hair was buzzed off, and she glimpsed tattoos peeking out from under the T-shirt sleeves.

"Well, this is a turnaround from the usual state of things," Derek remarked, sounding amused. "You know, *you* naked and covered in blood, me having to fetch and carry—"

"Just shut up and give me some pants, asshole."

Derek grinned and shoved a duffel into Ben's arms.

"There you go. The clothes are mine, so they're gonna be a little big on you, but it's better than running around bare-ass naked. And—" He held up a bag with a burger chain restaurant logo on it. "Brought you some meat."

"Derek, I could kiss you." The duffel gripped to his chest, Ben grabbed the bag with his free hand.

"No thanks, I'll pass. And on that topic, Gaby had me throw in some of her things too, since you said there was a woman with you." Derek turned to give Tessa a grin, flashing very white teeth. "Aren't you gonna introduce me? Sorry you have to deal with this jerkass and his lack of manners, lady."

"I was *getting* to that," Ben said through a mouthful; he already had the wrapper off a burger and had crammed a third of it into his mouth. "Tessa, this rude asshole is my friend Derek Ruger. Derek, this is my mate, Tessa."

Derek's eyebrows went up. "No shit? You didn't mention *that* part."

Tessa scrambled to her feet, realized she was holding a kitten, and put it quickly on the bed so she could hold out a hand. "Hi. It's nice to meet you. Thanks so much for helping us."

Derek clasped her hand in his. "Pleasure's all mine."

"Quit flirting with my mate, Ruger," Ben said as he set the duffel on the bed.

Derek laughed. "I've got a mate of my own at home, and a six-months-along bun in the oven. I just think she deserves some recognition for putting up with *you*."

Their easy rapport made Tessa feel shy. She used to think that she and Melody had a friendship like this, but now she was starting to think she'd never known Melody at all. She sat on the end of the bed and picked up a kitten to comfort herself while she watched Ben getting dressed in the loose workout clothes Derek had brought him.

"You want to bandage those before you bleed all over my best sweatshirt?" Derek asked. "I brought first-aid supplies."

Ben shook his head. "No, it'll heal up better if I don't cover it. It's partway there already. I just need protein and calories to finish the healing process." He started to unwrap another burger, paused, and held it out to Tessa. "Here. You haven't had anything yet."

"Thanks." She was able to muster up a smile for him, and set the kitten aside as she took the burger. She'd never had trouble hiding her feelings from anyone before, but Ben looked at her with a soft gaze that seemed to see right through her.

"Are you okay?" he asked.

Derek slapped him on his uninjured shoulder, making him wince. "Of course she's not okay, nitwit. There's a dragon hunting her. Seriously. What's your plan?"

"Don't really have one yet." With a last, concerned glance at Tessa, Ben sat on the edge of the bed and stiffly, one foot at a time, leaned forward to pull on socks. "The cabin's compromised. I'm not entirely sure how he found us."

"Ghost found me and Gaby at the cabin last year, too. Apparently," Derek said, reaching into the bag for a burger of his own, "your safehouse isn't as safe as you think it is."

"Ghost bugged your car, which is why I took special care to sweep mine. I really don't know how this guy tracked us down. The cabin's not in my name, and the only people who know about it are people who would never give me away." He turned, frowning, to look toward Tessa.

"What?" she said, startled. "You don't think I did something, do you?"

"No, of course not. I'd never think that. But do you mind if I see your necklace again?"

"Um ... I guess so." She fished it out of her T-shirt and this time slipped the chain over her head. It was still warm from her skin as she placed it gently in Ben's hand. She had to force herself to let go; she'd rarely taken it off since she'd opened the box and found it there, let alone given it to someone else.

"Huh." Derek leaned over to get a better look as Ben studied it. "What's that?"

"It's just a cheap crystal that my mother left me," Tessa said, feeling self-conscious. The necklace meant a great deal to her, but it was worthless to anyone else, at least as far as she knew. Her neck felt cool and bare without the chain around it.

"I'm starting to wonder about that." Ben held it up, twining the chain through his fingers. "Dragons always know where every piece of their hoard is located. At least that's what I've been told. Tessa, is there any chance this could have come from a dragon's hoard?"

"How would my parents get their hands on something from a dragon's hoard?"

"Could they have stolen it?" Derek asked.

Tessa wanted to laugh, but she couldn't manage it. "My parents weren't thieves!"

"How do you know?"

"Because they just ... weren't!" She fretfully tore off pieces of her hamburger bun. "I don't know much about them, I was only a few years old when they died, but my dad was some kind of salesman and my mom was a nurse. They were just ordinary people. They weren't thieves or spies or anything special."

"Maybe they didn't steal it," Derek suggested. "Maybe they found it."

Tessa gave him a flat look. "My parents just accidentally *found* something from a dragon's hoard. And put it in a safe deposit box for me."

"Hey," Derek said, "I'm just throwing ideas out there." He took a bite of his burger.

"It's not likely," Ben said. He turned the crystal over in his fingers. "I still think this might be how Reive found us, though. Unless you have anything else on you that might have been used to locate you."

Tessa shook her head. "Unless he visited my apartment and planted a tracking device in my suitcase."

"I didn't think of that," Ben said.

"I was joking!"

Ben leaned forward. "Tessa, they're obviously very committed to finding you. There's no telling what they'll be willing to do. Would you consider getting rid of the necklace?"

Tessa snatched it out of his hand, a surge of rage rushing through her. "No! It's mine!"

Ben and Derek exchanged a look, and Tessa felt her rage draining away as quickly as it had come. She opened her fingers to find she'd clenched her hand so tightly that the edges of the crystal had left red imprints in her skin.

"I'm sorry," she said. "I just can't stand the idea of not having it. It was my parents'. You probably don't understand how much that means to me, if you aren't close to yours. But it's all I have left."

"I know it's important to you," Ben said. "But ..." He reached out. "Can I hold it again?"

Tessa hesitated.

"I'm not going to take it away. I just want to hold it. I've never seen you like this about anything else."

"That's because I don't have anything else that means this much to me." She had an even harder time letting go this time. She trusted Ben, but there was still a tiny part of her that was irrationally afraid he'd take the necklace away for good.

"But you've only had this for two weeks, you said?"

"Two weeks, two days, it doesn't matter. It's from my parents. It's not special other than that."

"I'm not at all convinced that's true." Ben held the crystal up to the light. "I think there's something *very* special about this. I just don't know what. We need to show it to another dragon, Melody if we can find her, or—I hate to say this—my dad if we can't."

Tessa barely heard the last part; she'd almost forgotten that they'd last seen Melody engaged in battle with a much bigger dragon. "I really hope Melody's all right. It won't give away our location if we call her, will it?"

"I'm not going to worry about that," Ben said, making her realize he was just as worried as she was. "Do you want to call her? I think it might be better coming from you than me, in case she thinks I'm on Dad's side. Or do you have your phone?"

Tessa nodded. "It's in my pocket. May I have my necklace back? You said you weren't going to keep it."

Ben handed it back, with visible reluctance.

"I don't think it's hurting her in any way," Derek said quietly. "I mean, she looks fine."

"Maybe not, but it's definitely got its hooks in her somehow."

"You guys are imagining things," Tessa snapped. "It's *my* necklace. If there was anything magic about it, I'd know."

She tried calling Melody, but the call went to voicemail, so she sent a text: *Mel, thanks for the save, but we're worried! I'm with Ben. Call me.*

"Well, I guess that settles it." Ben sighed and swung his legs off the bed. "I need to take you to see Dad."

"Is your dad even going to let me in?" Tessa asked. "From everything you've said, about how he doesn't want to get involved—and if it's possible for them to *track* me somehow, we'll be getting him involved whether he wants it or not—"

"I don't care." Ben's eyes were hard as steel, and just a few shades darker. "You're my mate. I'm not giving him a choice about it."

Tessa set aside the other half of her burger; she'd lost her appetite. Two of the kittens converged on it. She caught them and held them in her lap, to their obvious displeasure.

They're hungry, she thought. *I can give them some of my left-over burger for now, but what they really need is to be taken some-where I can give them proper food and a litterbox.*

"How do you suppose your dad feels about cats?" she asked Ben.

The grin that spread slowly across Ben's face was a wicked one. "I don't know, but I can't *wait* to find out."

112

CHAPTER 11

I t had been a long time since Ben had traveled to his father's lair, but as they drove deeper into the mountains, down smaller and smaller roads, he was unsurprised to find out that he still vividly remembered the way. He might be only half dragon, and not enough to have gotten the dragon-shifting part, but certain things were stamped into his DNA. His dad was the head of their clan, and just as dragons could always find their hoards, a part of them would always yearn, like a compass needle pointing north, for home and clan.

Ben thought about his collection of exotic weapons back home. He didn't really think of it as a hoard, and he didn't seem to have the same quasi-mystical attachment to it that true dragons did to their hoards. But he still liked collecting things. And all his years of traveling around the world had left him feeling unpleasantly rootless, a feeling that hadn't gone away until he settled down again.

Some part of him was a dragon and would always be.

"I think I liked the mountains around your cabin better," Tessa said. They were driving up a ravine with walls of bare rock on either side that seemed to lean over the road. The sun was already low enough that the road was in shadow. "They're ... I don't know. Friendlier, somehow."

"So do I. But we won't be here for very long."

Assuming they were allowed to stay at all. Ben thought it was flattering Tessa had paid enough attention to the things he'd said about dragons, and about his dad, to grasp the nature of the problem. Her mere presence in his father's lair would suggest that Darius Keegan was trying to hide her from Reive's clan, possibly drawing them into all-out clan warfare. Darius was definitely not going to be happy about it.

But Ben didn't plan to give him a choice. He and Tessa were a package deal now. It was both of them, or neither.

He tried not to think about the possibility that his dad might go for the second option.

"Hey, Ben," Tessa said.

Ben glanced over at her. She'd changed into a pink sweatshirt from the bag of clothes Derek had brought them; it looked good on her. "Yeah?"

"Does Melody have a hoard?"

Melody still hadn't texted them back. Ben was trying very hard not to think about the implications. "Sure she does," he said. "She's a dragon. They all do."

"But I've been over to her apartment loads of times, and I never saw any sign of anything like that."

Ben smiled. "What were you expecting to see?"

"Well ... gold, and jewels? That kind of thing."

"All hoards are different," Ben said. "It's not about money. Dragons hoard the things they value. What does Melody like best, in all the world? What's her apartment full of?"

Tessa stared at him. A small furrow appeared between her brows. "Books?"

"Yep."

"She ... hoards *books*?"

"Yeah, you've been to her apartment, so you know what it looks like, right? Bookshelves all over the place."

"Wow," Tessa murmured. "What about your dad?"

"Ah. My dad's more of what you might call a traditional dragon. Gold and jewels and that kind of thing are exactly in his wheelhouse."

The car entered a tunnel; the world around them went black except for a row of lights guiding their way. "We're not going to a cave, are we?" Tessa asked nervously.

"It's a very tastefully appointed cave."

"You're joking, right?"

They came out of the tunnel and the setting sun lanced them both in the eyes. Tessa put up a hand to block it, and Ben slipped on a pair of sunglasses. "See for yourself," he said, and pointed.

They'd driven into a steep-sided valley, angled east-west and therefore collecting as much of the morning and evening sun as possible. His father's mansion was built high on the valley wall, perched at the top of a forbidding wall of rock. It was made of the same gray stone as the mountains, with red roofs that gleamed in the setting sun.

"So ... not a cave."

"No, not a cave. Though there is an extensive basement and wine cellar."

The road crossed the valley on a narrow bridge. For a few moments, a sunset-tinted lake glinted under them, dotted with small boats throwing dark reflections into its glasslike surface. Along the lakeshore, scattered lights glowed warmly at them through the gathering dusk.

"What's the economy here based on?" Tessa asked.

"Tourism, mostly. Lots of vacation homes and a few high-end hunting lodges. Everyone around here knows my dad as a reclusive billionaire. I guess they aren't wrong; they just don't know all the details."

Ben spoke to cover his own nervousness. He felt his panther growing restless inside his chest, reacting with a cat's instinctive unease at the presence of a larger, fiercer predator. Knowing intellectually that his father wouldn't hurt them (well, probably not) did little to calm the beast inside him.

The road forked, one branch going down to the lakeside and the small town near the bridge, the other switchbacking up the steep side of the valley toward his dad's estate. Ben drove past a series of PRIVATE PROPERTY - NO TRES-PASSING signs.

"This must be fun in the winter," Tessa remarked as Ben's car labored up an especially steep section of road.

"Not if you fly in and out."

Tessa glanced down into the valley. "I thought you said they—dragons—don't want to be discovered. Wouldn't people see?"

"Huh? ... oh, I see. No, he has a helipad and a private airstrip up there. I meant flying in the normal way."

Tessa gave a small, embarrassed laugh. "Oh."

"But you're not entirely wrong," Ben added. "The mountains behind my dad's estate are mostly wild land. My dad and my other dragon relatives shift and go hunting back there. I'd suggest not going outside at night."

"They wouldn't—"

"Hunt a human, no, of course not. Ethical considerations aside, their code of honor absolutely forbids it. But a human and a deer could look pretty similar from the air under a waning moon. So just ... stick to the house and gardens unless you have permission to leave."

Tessa shivered and nervously touched her parents' neck-lace through her sweatshirt. "If you're trying to be comfort-ing, let me tell you, it's not working."

Nice going, Ben's panther snarled at him. *I can smell how upset she is; can't you?* The panther was still on edge from proximity to the dragons' lair; Ben caught a flash of sharp, bared white teeth at the edge of his mind's eye.

His panther didn't have to lecture him; he felt guilty enough as it was. "I'm sorry," he said quietly, reaching out to clasp his hand over Tessa's. She turned her hand over and laced her icy fingers through his. "It's going to be okay— really, it is. I know your impression of dragons so far is probably pretty negative, but they're really just people, like any other people. And I'll be with you. I'm not going to let them hurt you."

This last statement was backed up by his panther's growl underneath his words. He wasn't sure if Tessa could hear it, but her fingers squeezed his tighter, and it felt as if her hand had warmed up somewhat.

The road leveled off at last. Trees blocked their view of the valley, or what could be seen of it in the growing darkness. They drove through a short stretch of woods and, as stars began to emerge in the purpling sky, came out onto the mansion's wide-open grounds.

He always forgot how big this place was. The house had seemed small from the valley floor, dwarfed by the height of the cliff and the massive scale of the mountains framing it, but now it loomed over them. Some of the windows were lit warmly from within; most were dark. Lights picked out a sweeping front drive. Ben drove past that to a row of garage doors in a separate outbuilding, and parked on the wide gravel apron in front of it.

A warm breeze rising up from the valley blew back their hair as they stepped out of the car. Tessa reached into the back to retrieve the kittens' tote.

"Leave that for now," Ben said. He knew she wasn't going to make the best impression on his dad, and he didn't give a damn, but if it was possible for her to meet his dad without having a large bright-blue Rubbermaid tote clutched in both hands, that would probably help.

Tessa shook her head firmly. In the tote, the kittens scratched and scrabbled. They'd been fed—he and Tessa had stopped to buy kitten food on the road—and had a nest in the tote made of Tessa's T-shirt and a spare sweatshirt of Derek's, but they were either nervous at the presence of dragons, or very ready to be out of the tote. Maybe both.

"They'll be okay for just a few minutes. We can talk to my dad and arrange for a room, and then come back and get them."

"No," Tessa said firmly. "They depend on me. I didn't leave them to be eaten by Reive, and I'm not leaving them now."

Ben couldn't help thinking that she was going to make a hell of a mom one of these days. Having been abandoned by her parents at an early age, intentionally or not, she'd brought all her protective instincts to bear on the other small, helpless creatures of the world.

"Okay, how about this. We'll take them inside—I know the layout of this place reasonably well, and we can pick any unused bedroom on this wing and—"

"Well, look what we have here."

The voice was gruff and deep; it sounded like its owner had been gargling with rocks. Ben sighed and turned around.

"Maddox. I liked you better in handcuffs."

The big, crewcut slab of muscle folded his arms, making his shoulders bulge and ripple under his suit. "You gonna try to arrest me again?"

"Not unless you do something illegal in front of me." Ben took a quiet sidestep to place himself between Tessa and his father's henchman. "We're here to see my dad."

"You call ahead?"

"I'm his son. I don't need an appointment."

"You sure about that?"

"Maddox, I know you don't like me, and trust me, it's mutual. But this is a matter of life and death. You want to make it a fight, go ahead; you'll answer to Dad for it." Ben nodded to Tessa. "Come on. Let's go in the house."

She glanced nervously at Maddox, but the big henchman made no threatening moves in their direction. When they started walking, he fell in line a few steps behind them, walking with startlingly silent steps for such a big guy—Ben could barely hear him at all, even on gravel.

Of course, it was hard to hear anything at all over the scrabbling, mewing kittens.

Tessa leaned forward to whisper, "Is he a dragon, too?"

"I don't think so." Ben glanced over his shoulder. Maddox's eyes glinted at him in the shadows. "He could be some other kind of shifter, though. Like me."

The gravel path, edged with ornamental shrubbery, curved gently around the verge of the driveway toward the big house. As they neared the steps leading up to the main entrance, the door opened and Ben's father came out.

At least he hadn't shown up as a dragon; Ben relaxed a little inside. He wouldn't put it past his father to do exactly that, probably scaring the life out of his mate when she'd just been attacked by a dragon on multiple occasions. And his father's shifted form was even bigger than Reive's.

Even as a human, though, Darius Keegan was an imposing man. Arms folded, he looked down at his son from the top of the steps. "What's this?" he asked flatly.

"You told me she needed protection. I'm protecting her." Ben was aware of Tessa giving him a quick look.

"I didn't tell you to bring her *here*."

"Where safer?" Ben asked succinctly. "Since you're not going to introduce yourself properly, Dad—Tessa, this is Darius Keegan, my father. Dad, this is Tessa Davelos."

He began to climb the stairs. Tessa, looking anxious, followed him after a moment of paralyzed hesitation.

Darius moved to block their path. "You dare to bring *that* into *my* house—"

"*She* is my mate."

Ben's panther rose up snarling in his chest. He was, he realized, spoiling for a fight. He hadn't gotten satisfaction with Reive, and then they'd been running, and his panther *hated* it, hated not having the opportunity to protect their mate properly. And this was a fight that had been coming for a long time.

"Do you want to challenge me on this, Father?" he asked, softly but with spring-wound steel underneath, aware of the panther rising to the surface, glinting gold in his eyes. "There is nowhere else safe for us. And we have an important piece of business we need to discuss. Important *dragon* business."

Darius's eyes flashed. "She knows?"

"We almost got killed by a dragon at my cabin," Ben said coldly. "I think she knows."

For a long moment they stood face to face, father and son. Ben's panther was tense inside him, barely contained, prepared to erupt out of him at the slightest threat to his mate.

Then, to Ben's surprise, his father stepped aside—not in a way that suggested capitulation but simply a sidestep as if he'd always meant to do that. "Take her to the Lilac Room. I'll be up shortly to talk."

Ben gave him a tight nod—one equal to another. The nod was not returned, but he thought his father's cold gray eyes viewed him now with a look he'd never seen there before. Assessing, but not in the usual way, when he was measured and found wanting.

He thought he might, for the first time in his life, have

earned a little of his father's respect ... long past the time in his life when he cared if he got it or not.

I don't want your respect, or your fatherhood. I just want to make sure you keep my mate safe. That's all.

As Ben and Tessa passed him, Darius stopped Tessa with a light touch on her arm. Ben and his panther both bristled; his fingers curled with the effort of keeping the cat in check. If his father made one move to harm her—

"What is that?" Darius asked. He tapped the plastic of the tote, causing a fresh eruption of scrabbling and mewing inside.

"Kittens?" Tessa said nervously.

"Kittens," Darius repeated. He seemed taken aback. Ben wasn't used to seeing his father caught off guard.

"They'll be in the Lilac Room with us," Ben told him. Flatly, a statement, not a question. That was the key to dealing with his father, one that he'd learned slowly over the years. Never show doubt or weakness; never give him a crack to sink his claws into. He rested a hand in the small of Tessa's back, making it clear to his father and Maddox and any other henchmen who might be watching from the shadows: *This is mine. She is mine. They are mine.* "Come on, Tessa," he added more gently. "Let's go. I'll show you where it is."

He was all too aware of his father's eyes on him as they turned away.

~

"He told you I needed protection? I thought it was Melody."

Tessa managed to wait until the door was closed and the two of them were alone (in a bedroom larger than her entire apartment) to say it.

"It came from Melody, by way of my dad. Do you want help with—"

"I've got it."

Ben had also offered to take the tote from her in the hall, but she'd stubbornly hung onto it, so now he merely watched as she set it in the middle of the cream-and-violet bedspread.

To her relief, the Lilac Room wasn't as overwhelmingly lavender as she'd been afraid of; it had a very tasteful blue, violet, and white color scheme. A bouquet of lilac flowers on the old-fashioned vanity looked so real that Tessa wanted to smell them to make sure they were, as she suspected, fabric. Surely they couldn't keep fresh flowers in all the rooms all the time, just in case a guest stopped by. But maybe they did; maybe that's what being *this* rich was all about.

She'd never felt as out of place as she did in this house. It was like she'd stepped onto the set of a movie. The public areas of the house were dominated by hallways with enormous high ceilings (to accommodate dragons, she thought, with an uncomfortable twist in her stomach), elaborate mosaics tiled in the marble floors, carved wooden moldings, and gilt wallpaper that she had an awful feeling might really be gold leaf. Ornate display tables held antique vases and abstract sculptures. She'd been terrified that she was going to bump into something with the cats' tote and knock over a vase worth several million dollars.

Meanwhile, Ben walked through it like he thought it was all perfectly normal.

Of course he did, she thought resentfully. He must have grown up with this. She knew it wasn't his fault, but that just made her feel more angry about being irrationally angry.

It was just ... what had happened to the guy she was slowly but steadily falling in love with? She hadn't known him for long, but she had thought she *did* know him. Ben was a down-to-earth guy, a guy who worked with his hands and built his own cabin, a dedicated cop. He was someone who, even if he hadn't lost his parents like she had, wasn't that close to them; he understood her feelings of alienation and isolation.

And now it felt like a whole new side of his world had opened up in front of her: something she hadn't even guessed at, which felt completely unwelcoming to her. It wasn't that Ben had done anything to make her unwelcome, it was just that she'd thought they had so much in common, and now she wondered if they'd ever had anything in common at all.

"Are you okay?" Ben asked, his voice gentle. He reached out a hand.

She pulled away. "I'm fine. I just need to make myself look —" *Less like me.* "—more presentable, that's all."

"There's a bathroom through there." Ben pointed to a white door with a gold handle. "Are you hungry? I can have the kitchen send something up—"

"No!" she snapped, temper flaring. He was just so *relaxed* about this, as if calling down to the kitchen for room service was a perfectly normal thing to do in a perfectly normal household. And she couldn't even think how to explain; anything she said would just make her sound stupid and childish. "Look after the kittens for me." And she went quickly into the bathroom before she either burst into tears or started yelling.

The bathroom was as stupidly, ridiculously huge and ostentatious as everything else in the house (*only* half *the size of my apartment*, she thought; *downright modest by their standards*) with an enormous step-down hot tub and a white vanity with a gold-edged mirror shaped like a giant shell. She did actually feel a little better once she'd washed her face with some of the faintly floral soap, dried her face on a towel with embroidered lilacs along the edge, and smoothed down her hair somewhat. She found a comb and other toiletries in a drawer of the vanity.

As completely over-the-top as this whole place was, it did feel nice to pamper herself a little bit. She wished she could just relax and enjoy the unaccustomed luxury.

The only person making you feel bad is you, she told herself firmly.

But as soon as she stepped out of the bathroom and saw Ben on the floor, playing with the kittens, she felt her level of tension start to ratchet up again. He'd taken off his shoes, and even in sweatpants a size too large for him, he looked at home there, in a way she never would be.

It's not like he's going to make you live in a mansion. It wouldn't even be bad if he did! I mean, you'd be in a mansion!

But ...

But there was still that sense of distance between them, that she hadn't felt until they came here.

Ben looked up at her and smiled hopefully. She managed to smile back, and sat down on the plush white carpet near him, picking up a kitten to pet it.

"Tessa," Ben said quietly, "if it's my dad, I promise you—"

"Stop," she said. "It's not—I mean—look, *you're* the one that wanted to come here." And that was the crux of the problem, really. Even telling herself that he was just trying to help didn't make her feel any better about it. "I'll let him look at my parents' necklace as long as I have your word that you won't let him take it away."

"I won't. I promise."

"I know." She softened, seeing how distressed he was, how much he wanted to make her feel better even though he didn't know what was bothering her. "It's just that ..."

She broke off, not sure how to explain, not sure if she even *could* explain. Ben started to reach out, gently, hand curled to brush her cheek with his fingers.

—at which point, the door opened without a warning knock and Darius Keegan loomed in the doorway. One of the kittens (Toblerone, of course) made a break for the hallway. Without pausing, possibly on pure instinct, Darius reached down in a smooth, lightning-fast grab and picked it up by the scruff as it ran past him. The kitten dangled in his grip, staring at him, while he stared at it.

"Don't hold them like that," Tessa said sharply, scrambling to her feet. "They get heavier as they get bigger, and you can't keep picking them up like they're tiny babies. You'll hurt him."

Ben made an abortive movement, as if he'd started to grab for her, and then he sat back on his heels, petting the kitten in his lap and silently watching.

Darius turned his flat, appraising stare from the dangling kitten to Tessa. "What?"

"You're holding it wrong. Look. I'll show you." As she took Toblerone out of his hands, there was a part of her shrieking, *He's a dragon! And you're just treating him like some random cat lady in the animal shelter!* He seemed to loom over her, terrible and tall, with a palpable sense of power surrounding him. No wonder the cats didn't like Melody and Reive. Tessa had never been able to feel this from the other dragons she'd met, but with Darius, she was all too aware of it. Lurking inside him was a huge predator, and it brought out the tiny skittering prey animal in the back of her brain.

But he was also *holding a kitten wrong*. Tessa cuddled Toblerone to her chest, calming him down. "Look," she said. "You have to support a cat and make sure it knows you aren't going to drop it. They don't like to be grabbed or just held out at arm's length like a bag of someone's trash. Would you?"

Out of the corner of her eye, she saw Ben staring at her in open awe. Darius was regarding her with a look she couldn't read at all. He looked a lot like Ben, she thought, but much sharper and harder, as if everything soft in him had been planed away. Ben's eyes were the gray of stormclouds and rain-washed seas; Darius's were the color of cold pewter.

Against her chest, the kitten had calmed and begun to purr. It was lucky it was Toblerone, she thought; a less outgoing kitten might have still been freaked out. This one might actually let Darius hold him.

"Look," Tessa said again, and lifted Toblerone carefully away from her chest. "Support its bottom with one hand, like this." She took Darius's cool fingers in hers and cupped them around the kitten's backside. "And with your other hand—no, baby—" Toblerone had begun to struggle. Tessa firmly clamped Darius's fingers around the kitten's chest, noticing that a hint of actual panic had slipped into his gunmetal eyes, and then let go and took a step back.

"Er," Darius said, now awkwardly holding a kitten. The kitten seemed no more pleased.

Tessa mimed bringing something to her chest. "Hold him against you, not at arm's length."

Very slowly, Darius brought the kitten to his chest. He was still holding it clamped firmly between his hands. "It appears to be trying to bite me."

Tessa rolled her eyes. "*Pet* it."

"I'm using both hands to hold it here," Darius pointed out reasonably.

"You don't need both hands now. Hold him to your chest with the hand under his chest. Then pet him with the other."

Darius cautiously ran his hand over the kitten's soft fur. Tessa held her breath in concern—she wasn't sure how Darius would react if the kitten clawed him—but Toblerone, true to his bold nature, seemed to be settling down.

Then he made a sudden break for freedom. Darius let go, startled, but instead of jumping down, the kitten clambered up his arm onto his shoulder. At the top, Toblerone paused and crouched, as if this wasn't quite what he'd had in mind but he couldn't think of a good way out of the situation.

Darius had much the same expression. He leaned his head away from the kitten and reached up cautiously to touch it.

Ben was staring.

Tessa decided that was about as much bonding as either of them could take, and stepped in to lift the cat off his shoulder; she had to stand on tiptoe. "Nicely done," she said with a somewhat forced smile. "And now you know how to pet a cat."

But he had lost interest in the cat as soon as he saw the silver chain around her neck. "Let me see it," he said.

It was a command, not a request. Darius Keegan, Tessa guessed, wasn't a man who was used to asking for things. At a different time, Tessa would have objected, but she didn't feel this was the time.

She set down Toblerone gently, and fished up the necklace out of her collar. As she slipped it over her head, she was intensely aware of the powerful sense of attraction she'd felt from the moment she had seen it among her parents' things. Giving it to Ben had been hard enough. Placing it in Darius's narrow palm was almost physically painful.

As soon as the crystal touched his skin, Darius made a soft, inhuman hissing sound. Tessa glanced quickly up at his face, and for a startling instant she glimpsed his eyes change. The pupils elongated to slits, and his eyes flashed green-gold before returning to normal gray human eyes so quickly she almost thought she'd imagined it.

Ben had seen as well. "It's draconic in origin, isn't it?"

"Yes," Darius said softly. He held the pendant up to the light, the silver chain twined about his long, strong fingers. "It is more than that, it is ... Benedict, will you leave the room, please?"

A few minutes ago, Tessa had been annoyed with Ben;

now she wanted to clutch at him to stop him from leaving. To her relief, he showed no signs of going anywhere. "I'm not leaving her alone with you."

"Oh, please." Darius raised his eyes heavenward. "What do you think I'm going to do?"

"To be honest, I have no idea. That's why I'm staying."

Darius closed his eyes in a slow blink. "We need to discuss dragon's business. You are not a dragon. So, leave."

Tessa knew Ben well enough by now to catch the sharp flash of hurt in his face. "Who cares?" she said heatedly. "I'm not a dragon either. And Ben's your son. Stop throwing in his face that he was born different from you. He couldn't help it."

"You know nothing of what you speak, human girl."

Tessa held out her hand. "If you won't say what you need to say in front of Ben, then give me my necklace back, and we'll go take our chances with Reive."

A muscle in Darius's jaw tightened. He gave Ben a sharp look. "This human is more troublesome than I expected."

"I know," Ben said with a trace of a smile.

"Very well." Darius placed the necklace back in Tessa's hand. For a moment of mingled hurt and relief, she thought he wanted them to leave, but then he seated himself in a chair beside the bed, showing no signs of going anywhere.

Tessa sat on the edge of the bed and slipped the necklace back over her head. It settled against her chest as if it had never been gone.

"Benedict," Darius began slowly, "have you ever heard of the Heart of the Hoard?"

"No," Ben said. He sat down beside Tessa and took her hand. She hesitated only a moment before leaning against him.

"No wonder. We only speak of it with other dragons." If Darius was aware of the flinch that Tessa felt in Ben, it didn't show on his face. "Every dragon has one. It's the first item in our hoard, the item around which all the rest accrue. It is, in some sense, our soul." He gave Ben a hard-to-read look. "You can see why we don't want non-dragons to know about it."

Tessa raised her hand to touch the crystal. She wondered, for the first time, if it was warm from Darius's palm or if it had its own inner heat. It had always felt warm when she'd touched it, but she had assumed it was heated by her skin. "And this is the heart of someone's hoard?"

"Not just any someone," Darius said. "A clan leader. Who did you say is after you?"

"He calls himself Reive Corcoran," Ben said.

Darius nodded slowly.

"You *do* know something about this," Ben said sharply. "Tell us."

"I need to do some research first," Darius said. Ben's anger slid off him like so much water.

"And then what?" Tessa asked. "Are you going to help us?"

Darius's thin-lipped smile was like a cool mockery of Ben's. "If another clan is searching for their own missing property, I will not stand in their way of reclaiming it. In fact, if this is indeed the Heart of another clan's hoard, I must upon my honor return it, and you, to them."

CHAPTER 12

"**T**hat bastard!" Ben fumed.

He was pacing the room, stalking from one side to another like a caged tiger. Or a caged panther. Tessa could almost see his twitching tail. He'd been seething ever since his father had left the room.

"He never promised to help us," she said, sitting on the bed with a kitten in her lap. "In fact, we came here knowing he probably wouldn't. And now we know what this thing is, at least."

"Not helping isn't the same thing as going out of his way to throw you to the wolves! Convenient, isn't it, this 'honor' of his? Can't help us when we ask, but if he can get involved just enough to screw us over, trust my dad to do exactly that."

"I don't know, Ben." Tessa turned the crystal over in her fingers thoughtfully before stuffing it down the neck of her borrowed sweatshirt. She tried to suppress a pang of loss at the thought of never having it again. "I think he actually is helping, in his way. Returning this where it came from is the right thing to do. Maybe if I explain to Reive that I inherited it from my parents and never saw it before, he'll just take it and go."

Ben stopped and turned abruptly around. "Letting you anywhere near Reive—"

"Is my decision," Tessa said.

"Well, *yes*, but Tessa, he's trying to kill you! You don't know what dragons are like, how hard-headed they can be—"

"I'm starting to wonder if the apple didn't fall very far from the tree."

That shut him up, but only for a moment. "What's that supposed to mean?"

"Ever since we came here ..." She raised her hands and let them fall in despair. The kitten jumped out of her lap. "Never mind."

"Tessa ..." Ben sat beside her on the bed. "If you want to leave, just say the word. We can leave the necklace here. It's even more likely now that the necklace is how Reive has been tracking you, and if my dad wants to return it so badly, let *him* deal with it."

Tessa didn't even notice she'd raised her hand to the necklace until she felt her fingers curl protectively around the hard lump of crystal under her sweatshirt. "And then what?" she asked defensively. "Live on the run? The only thing worse than knowing there's a dragon assassin after me is not knowing for sure until one lands on my front lawn."

Ben laid a hand on her leg. "I'm not trying to suggest—"

A brisk knock at the door interrupted him. Ben sighed and got up to answer it. Tessa took her hand off her chest. Getting rid of the thing would be the answer, wouldn't it? But why did she feel like that wouldn't solve her problems at all?

The person in the doorway was someone Tessa hadn't seen before, a middle-aged maid with a round, matronly figure, but a ramrod-straight back and military bearing. "The boss wanted me to tell you to dress for dinner. It'll be served in half an hour in the gold rotunda." She shoved a stack of clothing into Ben's arms.

"We're not interested—"

"Tell him thank you," Tessa interrupted.

The maid gave them both a brief nod and left.

"Tessa," Ben began.

"You don't make decisions for both of us." She stood up and reached for the clothes in his arms. "And I'm hungry. If we're going to be in this ridiculous mansion, I might as well get a good meal out of it. Let me see what he wants me to wear."

~

Ben wondered how it had all gotten so out of control. Tessa had clearly been upset ever since they'd gotten to his father's estate. He just couldn't figure out why. Everything he tried to do to smooth it over seemed to be making it worse.

But when she stepped out of the bathroom, where she had retreated to get ready, his breath caught in his throat.

Darius was a man with a lot of flaws, but he had an eye for aesthetics like no one Ben had ever met, and he knew in an instant that Darius had picked out the dress specifically with Tessa's coloring in mind. The coral and amber colors brought out the beautiful highlights in her warm, light brown skin; floating, layered skirts and a bodice with curling stitchery emphasized her curves. The dress left her shoulders bare, and though all she'd done was comb back her short hair and fix it in place with some spray, the effect was supermodel stunning. High coral-colored gloves covered the cat scratches on her arms.

She wore the necklace proudly and defiantly, the crystal nestling between the caramel mounds of her breasts.

Ben breathed a soft, "Wow."

Tessa's eyes had kindled warmly as soon as she saw him in his tux; she swept her approving gaze up and down his body. "You clean up nice, Detective Keegan."

"It's actually Lieutenant Keegan." He held out an arm, and she accepted it. "But you can call me Ben. You look amazing."

Tessa smiled and ducked her head. It was the first time they'd been truly easy with each other since they set foot in his father's house. "Is it really short for Benedict? I thought it was Benjamin."

"Now you know my deep dark secret." He smiled down at her. "And why I usually ask everyone at the precinct to call me Keegan. Dad claims it's an old family name, but I don't think that makes it any better."

"It's a good name. I like it." She squeezed his arm.

It was good to feel her warmth against his side, though he could also feel her tension. Trying to soothe her, he said, "Don't be nervous about dinner. It's not going to be *that* formal. I think Dad's just trying to intimidate us."

He could feel her going stiff and pulling away. "I'm not afraid."

"It's not that; it's just that I thought you might not be used to formal dining occasions—"

"Because I grew up in foster homes, rather than living in a mansion like your family?"

"Tessa," was all he could say, sudden awareness of the issue bothering her hitting him like a thunderbolt. She felt out of place here, strange and wrong; of *course* she would. He did, too. "Tessa, no, it's not like that—"

"I may not know much about fancy dining, as you so helpfully pointed out, but one thing I do know is that it's rude to be late," she said, and swept out the door in front of him.

Nice going, his panther helpfully contributed.

Shut up unless you can say something useful.

He caught up with Tessa outside the door, where she'd stopped because she clearly had no idea where to go. She took his arm without looking at him.

Ben started to open his mouth and then decided to let discretion be the better part of valor for the moment. It wasn't like they could have a private chat in the hallway, where servants or his father could come upon them at any moment. Later, he would have to reassure her.

As he led her through the mansion, he found himself noticing, with an outsider's eye, how easily he navigated the maze of the enormous house. No wonder she felt out of place. Ben remembered all too well what it had been like stepping into his house for the first time as an over-awed 13-year-old, trying to straighten his back and brush out the creases in the suit his mother had dressed him in. He had never even met his father as a young child, and as a teenager, he'd spent their ever-more-awkward visits trying desperately not to be the massive disappointment that he could tell his father thought he was.

It was only as an adult that he'd decided it didn't matter. He was never going to be the son his father wanted. He *couldn't* be. Darius didn't like him or care about him, and that was something he simply had to learn to live with. So he *had*; he'd built up a life he enjoyed, a career he liked. It had been empty without Tessa to fill his heart, but now he had her, too.

In your face, Dad. I never needed you at all.

But Tessa didn't know that. She saw him seemingly at home in all this opulence—it *ought* to look that way; he'd spent a lonely teenagehood desperately trying to play-act as

134

if he knew how to navigate his father's world, until the lie became reality. She must see herself as an outsider to his life, not as the true center of it, the one thing without which the rest of it would unravel.

Panthers might not have a hoard, as such, and therefore no Heart of it, but Tessa was *his* heart, and had been from the moment he'd met her. Maybe there was more dragon in him than he'd thought, except all he wanted to hoard was her.

And he didn't have the first clue how to tell her that, especially in this place that was so antithetical to who and what he was.

You could start by just, you know, telling her, his panther supplied.

It's not that easy in the human world.

Is it? his panther asked. *Or are you making it harder on yourself, and on her, than you have to?*

I could tell her in words, Ben thought at his panther, glancing down at Tessa's head so close to his shoulder, and yet so far away. *But she's been hurt so many times, and with this on top of everything, I don't know if she'll believe me. I have to show her.*

Somehow.

❧

Tessa was braced for still more over-the-top decorating ridiculousness in the dining room, and she wasn't wrong (were those *cherubs* on the walls? with gilt inlays? and who in the world needed a table that huge unless they were planning to feed an entire soccer team?) but it all washed out of her head when she saw who was already sitting at the table with Darius.

"Melody!" she cried. She pulled her hand out of the crook of Ben's arm and ran forward, stumbling until she realized she had to hold up these heavy skirts. She wasn't used to wearing dresses, let alone ones like this.

But Melody was already standing up, and the fact that she looked just as uncomfortable as Tessa felt (even though she wore a silver-and-black dress that, of course, made her look absolutely stunning) went a long way toward soothing Tessa's out-of-place feelings. Melody dropped a tiny silver fork to clatter on her plate and came to meet Tessa halfway across the expanse of marble floor—limping, Tessa couldn't help noticing. Melody winced as they hugged, and when Tessa pulled back, she saw bruises on the creamy expanse of her friend's chest above the dress's V-cut neckline.

"You're hurt!" Tessa said.

"I just took a few dings in the fight with Reive. It'll be healed by morning."

Melody slid her arm around Tessa's waist and the two women went to the table together. Darius was, of course, at the head of the table, and had already risen from his place to pull out the chair beside Melody, who had been seated at his left hand. Ben started to take the next chair down, beside Tessa, but Darius shook his head and gestured to the seat at his right hand.

Tessa was fully expecting Ben to simply go around and sit where indicated—a place was already set there, with a glass of wine—but Ben, with a small smile, sat in the chair he'd selected, far enough down the table that Darius would have to lean past Melody and Tessa to talk to him.

Darius clenched his teeth and made a peremptory gesture at a servant who had been hovering in the wings, so unobtrusive Tessa hadn't even noticed her until she hurried forward to move the glass of wine from the pre-selected spot to Ben's place.

To her relief, however, she found that sandwiched between Melody and Ben, she didn't feel quite as nervous as she had on the walk to the dining room. What was Darius going to do, turn into a dragon and try to eat her? If he did, it wouldn't even be the first time that kind of thing had happened to her today. And Melody was a dragon, too. She felt almost safe, for the first time today, with the two of them at her side.

"You didn't text me back," she murmured to Melody. "Don't scare me like that. I didn't know what Reive might have done to you."

"I'm sorry. I don't have my phone on me. It's been ..." She heaved a sigh. "... a day."

"You're telling me—"

Tessa jumped and broke off when the server appeared at her elbow, placing a small silver dish in front of each of them. The dishes each contained a single tiny tart, drizzled with chocolate and just large enough to accommodate a single blackberry on top. "Compliments of the chef," the server murmured.

Tessa stared at the tart and wondered how you were supposed to eat that. Pick it up? But she'd get chocolate on her gloves. Cut it up? Stab it on the end of a fork? Was this some kind of etiquette test?

She surreptitiously snuck a peek at the others to see what they were doing, just in time to see Melody reach for her fork and miss on the first try. Tessa had been so distracted with everything else that it had taken her this long to notice that Melody, for the first time since Tessa had known her, wasn't wearing her glasses.

Tessa leaned close enough to whisper, "Don't be a vain goose. You're blind as a bat without your glasses. I've known you long enough to know *that*."

"Dad doesn't like them," Melody whispered back. "He thinks they look unrefined."

Darius and Ben were oblivious to the women's whispered

conversation; they were too busy having a staring competition down the length of the table as Darius sipped on his wine and Ben blatantly ignored the hint to pick up his own glass.

"So what? It's *your* face. Do you always eat dinner with your dad just having to guess where everything is?"

"I normally have my contact lenses with me. This time I left in kind of a hurry and didn't have time to pack."

"So put the glasses on. You fought a dragon today; the least you can do is not accidentally stab yourself with your own fork."

Melody opened her mouth to argue, and then closed it. "You know what?" she said. "You're right." She reached under a fold of her silver-and-black skirts. There was a little rustling as she undid a hidden pocket, and a moment later she slipped her glasses onto her nose. Now the effect was much less "stunning debutante" and more "librarian dressed up for a library function."

Tessa found it a vast relief. She looked so much more like Melody that way: still very pretty, but in the usual Melody kind of way. It made Tessa wonder if the reason why Melody normally tried to make herself look as dowdy as possible was because every time she was around her father, she had to deal with being forced into the role of elegant firstborn daughter, and it didn't suit her.

Melody gave Tessa a quick, conspiratorial smile, and quietly carved off a bite of her tart, this time hitting it perfectly on the first try. Darius turned to look at her, mouth open to say something—then stopped, and looked again, longer.

Tessa waited with bated breath for him to say something about the glasses. Oh, she couldn't *wait*. She had so many things to say to *him* about the way he treated his children.

As if he could sense Tessa's pent-up urge to unload on

him, Darius kept his thoughts to himself and merely took a sip of his wine.

Melody kept her gaze on her plate as she ate her tart in tiny bites. Ben was idly stabbing his with his fork, over and over, as if he planned to kill it with a thousand tiny puncture wounds.

Tessa cut her tart in half with her fork and sampled it. She wasn't impressed; the flavor was bland, stuck somewhere between sweet and savory. Though maybe it was the tense air at the table sucking the flavor out of everything.

A soup course came around, served in wide shallow bowls that seemed designed to tip into a person's lap. Tessa watched Melody so she knew which spoon to pick up from the complex place setting, and poked at the soup carefully. It seemed to be some kind of seafood. She took a cautious sip. It was good, delicately flavored and just a little spicy, though slightly on the cool side for her taste.

"This is a traditional family recipe from the old country," Darius remarked in a mild tone that nevertheless carried all the way down the table. "It's said that back in my grandfather's time, if someone offended one of the old dragon clans, their punishment was to be made into a broth and served to the clan in this style."

Tessa dropped her spoon.

"For *fuck's sake*, Dad," Ben snapped. "Are you capable of at least *acting* like a civilized person for as long as it takes to—"

"May I have the recipe?" Tessa asked loudly.

This was followed by a silence so profound that the sound of a servant's foot scuffling in the hallway seemed very loud.

"After all," Tessa went on, "I'm dating your son, so I need to learn his family traditions." She forced herself to lift a spoonful of the soup to her lips, all the while staring at Darius and chanting in her head, *It's only seafood, it's only seafood.* "And," she added, wiping her lips with her napkin, "I want to know how to behave properly if someone offends me."

She followed this up with another stare at Darius. His face was completely blank. So was Melody's. Tessa didn't even want to look at Ben.

And ... now is the point when Ben's father transforms into a dragon and eats me in front of his entire family. This day is going great. *At least now I know I'll be served in a tasty broth.*

Then Darius laughed.

"Perhaps this one is, after all, a suitable mate for a dragon," he declared, pointing at Tessa with his spoon. "Is the soup to your liking, or would you prefer a different course?"

"The soup is entirely to my liking," she said, dipping her spoon again for another bite, this time with only a minimal amount of jaw-clenching. *It's only seafood ...* "And I was *very* serious about wanting the recipe."

"I'll have it send to your room. Er ... where those animals still remain, I presume."

"Oh yes, that's another thing," Tessa said. "We need a litterbox. They've probably already taken a dump or two on your nice white carpet, most likely under the bed. There's kitten food in the car, by the way. They'll need that too."

She delivered all of this in her best approximation of the peremptory tones Darius had used on them earlier. *Okay, NOW is when I get eaten ...*

But the thing was, she thought she knew how to deal with people like Darius. The ones she was used to weren't dragons. They were customers who wanted *this exact cat* even though the information packet clearly stated "No homes with small children" and there were half a dozen small children clinging to them but *I'm paying for this cat and I want this one!* They were social services workers who held her teenage life in their hands and thought they knew what was best for her better than she did.

You didn't back down, didn't show weakness, and didn't yell. You just planted your feet and told them what they were going to do. If you made yourself impossible to move, most people got tired of trying to move you and went around instead.

Darius smiled slightly and turned his head. "Malva? You heard her instructions. Please relay them to Maddox. I'm sure he'll enjoy it."

"You're just trying to make that guy hate my guts, aren't you, Dad?" Ben said, with a levity in his voice that Tessa knew him well enough to know was forced. But he seemed a little less tense than earlier. He brushed the backs of his fingers against her bare shoulder.

"You've shown that you're perfectly capable of annoying him yourself," Darius said. He leaned back in his chair and steepled his fingers as another course was brought around, this time a flaky fish garnished with parsley and lemon. "And I thought you'd outgrown dragging me into your messes whenever you get in a scrape."

"That's rich, coming from you, when you're the one who got me involved in the first place." Ben slipped his hand down to rest on Tessa's gloved forearm. "Plus, if an assassin hunting my mate and nearly killing my sister is what you call a 'scrape,' I don't want to find out your idea of a serious problem. So how is your 'research' going so far?"

Darius considered them over his steepled fingers and then picked up his fork. "Reive's clan leader is his great-uncle, Heikon Corcoran. Intriguingly enough, the family's gone through some upheaval in the last couple of decades. Heikon was deposed in a coup orchestrated by his younger brother Braun—Reive's grandfather. Several other members of the clan were in on it, including Reive's father. Recently, within the last couple of years, Heikon reclaimed his place at the top of the clan and had the conspirators executed."

"You got all of this in an *hour*?" Tessa said.

"He knew some of it already," Ben murmured.

Darius smiled as he dug his fork into the fish. "The key to being well connected, Miss Davelos, is knowing exactly who to call for the latest gossip ... and one never reveals one's sources. Eat up, it's wild-caught salmon. Very good for you. Full of omega-3."

"Anyway, fascinating dragon politics aside," Ben said, "what does all of this have to do with Tessa?"

Melody spoke up in her soft voice. "Do you think Tessa's parents knew the Corcorans?"

"Where are you from, Miss Davelos?" Darius asked her. "Originally, I mean. You needn't be specific; the state will do."

"We lived in Colorado when I was small. That's where my parents died."

Darius nodded. "And that's where Heikon Corcoran has his lair."

"Oh," Tessa said. It was a small, soft sound.

"If the Corcorans believe Tessa's parents stole part of their hoard," Darius said, "that would explain why they're hunting her."

"They didn't!" Tessa flared, closing her fingers over the stone. "My parents *weren't* thieves. They weren't."

"Merely a suggestion," Darius said mildly. He went on eating.

There was a throat-clearing noise and Maddox loomed very suddenly at Darius's shoulder. Tessa still didn't know how he could move around so quietly, but she took some satisfaction from the cat scratches on the backs of his hands. He leaned down to murmur into Darius's ear.

Darius nodded, murmured back, and Maddox left as

quietly as he'd come. Darius continued eating, oblivious, it seemed, to all the eyes at the table fixed on him.

Finally Ben said, "What was that about?"

Darius raised a hand until he had finished chewing. "It seems," he said after swallowing, "that your assassin is here."

Melody fumbled her napkin and dropped it in her lap. Ben threw a protective arm around Tessa. "And you're just mentioning this *now*?" he snapped.

"I've given Maddox instructions not to let him in. That being said," Darius added, raising his head to fix Ben and Tessa with a cool stare, "my business plans do *not* currently include a feud with the Corcorans. I am not sheltering you. However, the meal will be spoiled if we leave it to cool while we deal with this."

Everyone else at the table stood up, pointedly.

"Ah, well." Darius sighed and laid his napkin beside his plate. "Perhaps the leftovers can feed your infernal cats."

"You should go somewhere safe," Ben told Tessa quietly. "Go back to our room and wait for me. I'll talk to Reive. Maybe we can come to some kind of agreement."

Tessa shook her head. "I need to be there. I'm not letting you negotiate with Reive on my behalf." *Or go into danger without me.*

"Tessa." Melody reached for her friend's hand, black-gloved fingers slipping into coral. "In this, he's right. It would be too easy for Reive to simply shift and grab you. I'm not sure if I could stop him. I'm not sure if Dad *would* stop him."

Ben lightly kissed the corner of Tessa's mouth. "Go with her, love. She'll protect you."

A shudder went through her. It was the first time either of them had spoken the word *love* aloud. She wanted to say it back to him, but it was as if her throat was paralyzed; the words wouldn't come.

And then Ben was turning away with his father, and the

moment had slipped away. Tessa strained after him, but Melody's hand, strong and implacable, pulled her in the other direction.

How had she never noticed how strong Melody was before?

"Let them go," Melody murmured. "I know a balcony where we can watch. We can see and hear them, but they won't see us."

Tessa nodded and tore her eyes away from Ben's back. Before leaving the table, she turned around to fork up a last large bite of the fish and cram it into her mouth. It *was* very good fish, and she was still hungry.

She tried not to think of it as her last meal.

CHAPTER 13

As Ben, together with his father, stepped out of the wide double doors of the mansion's main entrance, the first thing he saw was Reive's motorcycle, not looking any the worse for wear after its adventure in the creek, parked in the sweeping front drive. Reive stood at the bottom of the steps, looking up with his hands shoved into the pockets of his black leather jacket and the night wind from the valley ruffling his dark hair.

Reive hadn't come any further because Maddox stood at the top of the steps, arms folded and wide shoulders bulging at the seams of his suit.

Ben had a feeling that Reive could have taken Maddox easily—whatever Maddox shifted into, it probably couldn't beat a dragon—but hadn't tried for the same reason that Darius hadn't run Reive off yet. The state of relations between the different dragon clans was fragile. None of them wanted to be the one to break the peace.

"Reive Corcoran," Darius said. He glided forward, and Maddox moved out of the way. "To what do I owe the pleasure of this visit?"

"I think you know," Reive said. He stood with his legs apart, body loose but tense, ready to move if he had to. "I'm here on behalf of my clan. I believe you have something that belongs to us."

Ben had to stop himself from looking up at the mansion, trying to figure out which of the lighted windows belonged to the Lilac Room.

"Ah yes, the girl with the rather important necklace," Darius said. "I'll turn her over to you in just a moment, although—"

"The hell you will!" Ben shouldered his way between his father and Maddox. His cat was snarling inside him, struggling to push its way out and claw at this threat to their mate. "She's not yours to give, and she's not going anywhere."

"She's not mine to conceal, either," Darius pointed out mildly. "May I ask why you want her, Reive of clan Corcoran?"

"She's a thief and a traitor," Reive said.

"She is none of those things!" Ben snarled. "She'd never heard of dragons until I told her about them. She didn't even know what her necklace *was*. She's blameless in all of this."

"Not my call." Reive sounded regretful, though Ben couldn't exactly muster up sympathy for him. "I'm under orders from my clan leader. Just give me the girl and we can all—"

"Orders to do *what*?" Ben demanded. "To kill the person who has the necklace, regardless of who it is or how they got it? Does your *honor* permit you to go around killing random bystanders who just happened to get their hands on a piece of jewelry when they don't even know what it's *for*?"

Reive gave a short, humorless laugh. "It doesn't work like that, trust me. The person who has the necklace is the only person who *could* have the necklace. Which means she's guilty, sad to say." He looked up at Darius. "You're Darius Keegan, the head of this clan, correct?"

"That is correct," Darius said.

"You can stonewall me, and you can negotiate for the girl's life with my clan head if you want to go that far out on a limb, but it won't change the outcome. Trust me, my clan leader is not the type to change his mind on a whim."

"Nor am I," Darius said with a trace of a smile. "He's right, Benedict. This is a matter of honor. You'll recover from the loss of your mate; she's only a human—"

"Reive Corcoran, I challenge you to a duel," Ben said.

There was a moment's pause, when the only sound was the wind rustling the leaves of the trees along the edge of the cliff, and then Reive said, "Pardon?"

"A duel. I challenge you to combat, me and you. I may not be a dragon," Ben said, with a hard look in his father's direction, "but I grew up around them, and I know how dragon culture works. All of you live your lives according to ages-old traditions, and one of those traditions is the resolution of disputes between clans in single combat. Father? Am I wrong?"

"It ... has been done," Darius admitted. "But this isn't a matter between our clan and theirs. It's strictly between you and them."

"It's a matter for the clan *now*. Since I brought her here. At least, Heikon Corcoran could easily see it as one."

Darius's eyes flashed; Ben glimpsed his father's dragon for an instant. "You played me."

"No, I didn't. I hoped you'd *help* me, because I'm your son and I do still believe, deep down, that means something to you. But since you won't, this is the only path you've left me." Turning to look down the steps at Reive, Ben called, "Do you accept my challenge? Just between you and me, I don't think you *want* to kill her. Give her a chance to escape with your clan's honor intact."

Reive took his hands out of his pockets; he wore fingerless leather driving gloves. "Or I'll simply kill both of you. There's no honor in this. A mere panther shifter against a dragon? That fight will be over in moments. I refuse."

"So what would make it honorable?" Ben asked, his heart beating heavily. "What if we agree to fight in our unshifted bodies? You against me, human-form? We're about the same size. You couldn't ask for a more level playing field."

"Dragons are still stronger," Reive said. He smiled faintly, an expression that made Ben think of his father. "And I don't know how long I can contain my beast once I really let myself go."

"I don't either." Ben could already feel his panther struggling inside him, wanting to be let out to claw that smirk off Reive's face. "So we'll fight as humans for as long as we can keep our beasts leashed. And then it's panther against dragon —but not if I defeat you first."

"This will not be a fight to first blood," Reive said, his voice cool. "I know my clan head won't accept that. It will be a fight to serious injury at the very least. Perhaps to the death."

"I know," Ben said. He didn't look at his father, and forced himself not to worry about Tessa. *If I lose, Melody will protect her. She's already proven that she's willing to defy draconic honor and Dad's orders to help us.*

"Then I accept," Reive said quietly. He stripped off his jacket and slung it across the motorcycle's seat.

∼

"We can't let him do this! He'll be killed!"

On a glassed-in balcony high above the action happening below, Melody caught her friend to prevent Tessa from throwing open the sliding glass doors and screaming her rage at the men below. "Tessa, stop! If you show yourself, there's nothing to stop him from shifting and taking you back to his clan for execution. Or simply flying you high into the air and letting you fall to dash your brains out on rocks in the valley. He's your *executioner*, don't you understand?"

"I don't care!" Tessa cried wildly, struggling against Melody's powerful grip. "Let him! At least that way Ben won't have to fight him and die!"

"Listen!" Melody gave her a shake and gripped both Tessa's upper arms, turning the other woman to face her. "Think of it as Ben buying time for us to find another solution, one in which no one has to die. *Think!*"

Tessa took a few deep breaths, forcing herself to calm down. What *could* they do? Who could stop this? Her father clearly wouldn't. And there was only one other authority she could think of to appeal to.

"Can we somehow get in touch with the head of the Corcorans?" she asked Melody. "This Heikon guy."

"I ... don't know." Melody hesitated, some of her usual mousiness creeping back into her manner. "I don't know if he'd talk to us."

"But we're in your father's house, right? What if he thought your father was calling him? I don't know how all of this works, but I guess it'd be like the leader of another country calling our President, right? He couldn't *not* take the call."

"Well, sort of," Melody admitted. "But we still have to find out *where* to call, and—"

"So let's get moving! Your dad was just looking into the Corcorans, so there should be somewhere around here that we could go to get their number and all that other useful information, right? Where would that be?"

"His office," Melody said immediately. "I can take you there."

Tessa looked down at the drive, and her throat tightened at the sight of Ben and Reive squaring off against each other. It looked like they were going to fight right there. They'd both shed their jackets, and Ben had taken off his shoulder holster.

Please don't die, she thought as she turned away to hurry after Melody. *Please hold on. You can win this fight, I believe in you—but if it doesn't work, we need a backup plan.*

I'll find something. I promise.

I love you.

CHAPTER 14

Darius stood like a statue as Ben stripped off his tuxedo jacket and slung it over a marble bench, followed by his holster and gun.

"As the challenger," Reive called up the steps, "I choose the weapon."

Weapons. Right. Too much to hope that they'd fight bare-handed. "I agree," Ben called down. "What do you choose?"

"Knives."

Ouch. But it was a good choice, the closest human alternative to the claws that were the natural weapon of both dragons and panthers.

Maddox looked toward Darius, who gave a slight nod, face like stone. The henchman drew two knives from somewhere under his jacket and tossed one toward each of the combatants.

Shifter-quick reflexes were more than enough to pluck a knife out of the air. Ben caught it easily and hefted it, feeling its weight and balance. It was a good knife, and a big one, the size of a kitchen butcher knife and razor-sharp along the gleaming edge. Down at the bottom of the stairs, Reive did a few test thrusts and tossed the knife from hand to hand.

"I have one question for you, Benedict," Darius said, turning toward him. "Can you win this?"

"I have to," Ben said. "For Tessa."

Darius scowled. "That's not the answer I was hoping for."

"Yeah, well, me not being a proper part of the clan is a sword that cuts both ways, isn't it? You can't order me to do anything."

Darius's dragon flashed in his eyes. "I could stop you."

"Yeah. You could. But you'll have to do it by force." Ben met his father's stony gaze. "Dad ... for once in your damn life, *trust* me. Trust me to be able to do this."

Darius looked away.

"Ready?" Reive called up the stairs.

"Yeah." Knife held loosely in one hand, Ben walked past his father and Maddox, down the stairs.

Up close, Reive looked troubled. He was younger than Ben had realized, probably only in his mid to late 20s—and that was likely his real age, too; the sharpness of feature that defined older dragons wasn't there in his face yet. "You don't have to do this," Reive said. "All you have to do is stand aside—"

"Or *you* could stand aside."

"I can't." Reive smiled slightly. "Honor."

"I know. I may not be a dragon, but as a man in love, I have my own kind of honor." Ben raised the knife in a salute. "I don't want to kill you, but you will not pass me."

"And I don't want to kill you, but if you won't stand aside, I must." Reive returned the salute, and they stood stock-still, both watching each other.

Ben hoped Tessa wasn't watching from the house. He didn't want her to see this.

"Begin," Darius called.

~

M elody unlocked the door to Darius's office with a large, old-fashioned brass key.

"I'm not in here very often," she said as she stepped inside and turned on the lights. "Occasionally he has me do some business stuff for him. I don't know if Ben told you, but Dad is ... well ... he's basically a mobster. He has some legitimate business interests, and some that are very much not. I mostly stay out of the illegal stuff if I can."

Tessa looked around, impressed despite the urgency and fear beating at the back of her brain. Darius's office was enormous, with high enough ceilings that he could probably have transformed in here, and tall windows looking down on the night-cloaked valley.

The office's furnishings were an interesting mix of old and new. The huge oak desk looked like an antique, as did the polished wooden cabinets and bookshelves along the walls. But there was also a large flatscreen monitor on the desk and all the usual home office equipment, a printer and fax machine and so forth, ergonomically arranged in cabinets near the desk.

Melody tapped a key to wake the computer up and typed in a password. "Most of his files are on paper. My dad doesn't quite trust computers. If he was really looking into the Corcorans, there should be a file on them around here somewhere. He might have already put it away. He's very organized."

No kidding. The top of the desk was almost painfully tidy; besides the computer, it contained nothing except a gold fountain pen in a polished cherry holder, a small desk calendar, and, adding a personal touch, a framed photo of a young Melody looking chubby and unhappy in a dress much too fancy for a small girl. No pictures of Ben as far as Tessa could see.

But right now Darius's lousy parenting wasn't her first concern. She pulled open all the unlocked filing cabinet drawers that she could find. Melody came behind her and unlocked the rest of them with a tiny key. The number of filing cabinets staggered and dismayed her. And those weren't even all the files; there were shelves full of leather binders too. Tessa pulled one down and opened it. The yellowed papers inside looked like they were from the middle of the previous century.

"Keep in mind," Melody said, kneeling to pull out a long row of files from the bottom shelf of a cabinet, "Dad's been running the clan for over a hundred years, and his business interests for longer than that. There is a lot of information here. We can't possibly get through all of it in time. Just look for something in the C's that looks like it was recently opened."

"Did you say a *hundred* years? How long do dragons live?" Tessa asked. She shoved the binder back onto its shelf and went back to pawing through filing cabinets.

"Several hundred years, if we don't find a mate. Or so I hear. Dad doesn't believe most dragons have mates. He wasn't mated to either my mother or Ben's mom, and they're not still together."

"What happens if they—if you find a mate?"

Melody pulled down a stack of binders, coughing as dust settled on her dark hair. Her black gloves were dusted with it, as if she'd dipped her hands in flour. "Our lifespan adjusts itself to match our mate's. They get a little longer lived, and we get a little shorter lived. At least that's what I've been told —Aha!"

She triumphantly held out a file folder toward Tessa. "Here we go. And it's been recently updated. Look, he's got

Heikon Corcoran's email address and phone number. C'mon, let's see if we can Skype him."

"We're going to Skype with a dragon?" Tessa asked in disbelief as Melody hustled them both back to the computer and dropped into the big, padded leather chair.

"Dragons, the older ones, *love* Skype. I think the really traditional ones, like my dad, never quite got used to talking to people on the telephone. Being able to talk face-to-face over long distances is perfect for them. Just like how things were in the old days, except better." She brought up the program. "Okay, let's see if this just gets us a secretary or something, or—"

The window expanded to fill the screen, and suddenly they were looking at a man sitting at a desk very like Darius's, but more cluttered and less organized.

Tessa, standing behind Melody's chair and slightly out of the camera's main field of view, thought she could see the resemblance to Reive very clearly. This man had the same high cheekbones and clear dark eyes. He was old enough for his hair to be iron-gray rather than glossy black like Reive's. Given what Melody had said about how long dragons lived, Tessa wondered how long one of them had to live in order to visibly begin showing signs of age. Darius had a sort of ageless quality about him; he looked somewhere in his 40s, but could have been well-kept 50s or *very* well-kept 60s. Since he was Ben's father, Tessa had automatically assumed that he was somewhere on the higher end of the age scale. Now she wondered how many more years he would go on looking like he was 45. A century? Two?

But she realized as this stranger turned toward the camera that it wasn't just the resemblance to Reive that made him look familiar. A memory surged out of the murky darkness at the back of her head, where her dim, fragmentary early-childhood memories of her parents lived. She'd seen this man before. She thought he might have held her in his lap, once, a long time ago ...

"Darius Keegan? How unexpected. It's been some time—" Heikon broke off. "Who are you?"

"I'm Melody Keegan, Darius's daughter. But I'm not the person who wants to talk to you." Melody rolled the chair to the side, so Tessa could move into the camera's field of view.

Heikon jerked back as if he'd been struck. "Harriet," he breathed.

Hearing that voice was like a cool wind from the past blowing across her soul. "No," Tessa said. "I'm Tessa. Harriet was my mother."

"Yes," Heikon said quietly. "Yes, of course ... she would be so much older now. I forget how short-lived humans are. That's right, Harriet and Peter had a child, didn't they? I had forgotten. It's amazing; you are her very image. You could *be* your mother, child."

"Oh," Tessa whispered. "I didn't know."

Beyond some dim childhood recollections, she had seen pictures of her mother for the first time in the family photos from her parents' box of things. But she had never connected her mother's face with the one she saw in the mirror. Her mother was beautiful, with smooth brown skin and laughing eyes.

But before she could open her mouth to ask more questions, Heikon's face hardened. "As you're calling me from Darius Keegan's account, I assume your family has sought sanctuary with him. From all I've heard of him, I'm surprised he's granted it—"

"My brother, Darius's son, is her mate," Melody said.

"Really? Well," he sighed, "that's certainly a complication I didn't need."

"And that's why I'm calling you!" Tessa said. "My mate is holding off Reive right now. You have to call Reive off."

"And why should I do that, child?" Heikon sounded, in that moment, old and inutterably weary.

"Because Reive is going to kill him!"

"From what you're telling me, the only reason why Darius's son is in danger is because he put himself there."

"For me!" Tessa cried. She took off the necklace and held it up, dangling the crystal in front of the computer's camera. "Look, if you want this, *take* it! I don't need it! None of it is worth any of this. Just take your stupid Heart of the Hoard or whatever it's called and go *away*—"

She stopped because Heikon was laughing, a soft laugh with a bitter edge.

"The Heart of the Hoard, you said?"

"Yes!" She shook the chain, making the crystal dance and catch the light. "This!"

"Ah, I regret to tell you, your parents did a poor job of explaining the situation to you. Put that bauble back on."

"I don't want it! I'll drop it in the mail right now if you'll tell me where to send it to. Or I'll give it to Reive to take back to you."

"You still don't understand," Heikon said, and his voice had become curiously gentle. "The Heart of the Corcoran Hoard is not a rock, child. The Heart of the Hoard is *you*."

~

At Darius's signal, Reive sprang into motion, leaping forward with the knife held low.

Ben wasn't there; he'd already sidestepped lightly, relying on his animal's speed and reflexes. He drove the knife in from behind, but Reive was already dodging out of reach.

Let me at him! Ben's panther snarled.

No. I need your speed, but this is a fight for humans. If we shift, he'll shift too, and we'll lose.

His panther snarled wordlessly. Such nuances were beyond its understanding. It only knew that its enemy, the man who threatened their mate, was *right there*. And it knew its claws and teeth were more than a match for his soft, human body.

He's a dragon, you feline fool. Ben had to devote precious concentration to holding his cat in check as he and Reive fought their way across the wide driveway and onto the lawn, ducking and dodging and, once, parrying in a clash of sparks and a shriek of metal on metal. *You can't win against a dragon. We can't win. The only chance we've got is if he, and we, stay human-shaped.*

He could tell by the look of intense concentration on Reive's face that his opponent was fighting a similar battle with his animal. Ben could only hope Reive's dragon wasn't even harder to control than his cat.

They seemed to be evenly matched. Reive was slightly faster and seemed to have more familiarity with the knife as an offensive weapon; Ben guessed that he'd trained with it, perhaps formally, which was probably why he'd requested it as a weapon. Ben's own knifework was a rudimentary smattering of tricks he'd picked up over the years. But he had the advantage of fighting experience in general. Reive was well trained, but relatively inexperienced. Through years of traveling in rough parts of the world, and then in his work as a cop, Ben had gotten in fistfights, knife fights, gunfights, and just about every other kind of fight. And they both were similar in size and reach.

When two combatants were this closely matched, it was going to be a battle of mistakes. Whoever slipped up first would lose. And this thought had just crossed Ben's mind when a moment's inattention sent his foot skidding out from under him on the dew-slick grass. He managed to thrust wildly upward and turn Reive's knife aside where it would have plunged into his chest, but it opened a long cut along Ben's arm.

Reive clearly hadn't been expecting it to go like that, and staggered off balance, stumbling backward just long enough for Ben to regain his feet. For a moment, they stood some ten feet apart, eyeing each other. Blood trickled down Ben's arm and dripped on the grass, making his grip on the knife slippery. He considered switching it to the other hand, but he wasn't left-handed; he would be at a severe disadvantage.

"Know that I regret this," Reive said.

"I haven't lost yet, asshole," Ben growled, and launched himself forward.

Reive moved to intercept, but met nothing but empty air; the attack had been a feint. Instead Ben dodged toward Reive's unguarded side. Rather than stabbing, he plunged his elbow into Reive's ribs, knocking the wind out of him, and followed it up with a punch to the side of the head. Reive managed to twist away so he only caught the edge of Ben's fist, but now he was the one breathing hard and reeling as they parted again.

The cut on Ben's arm stung and itched as his healing factor worked on it. The bleeding had already stopped. But his body was still recovering from his injuries earlier that day. His shoulder felt sticky; he guessed the healing cuts had been torn open by the exertion.

His panther was half frantic. *Let me at him!*

And then we'll die, cat. We have to do this together: my human hands and mind, your speed and reflexes.

I'd prefer claws and teeth, the panther sulked.

This is too important for your feline pride, Ben told his cat. *We must win for our mate. For Tessa.*

For Tessa, the cat echoed, and he could feel a settling in his chest, the panther no longer fighting him but working with him instead. Its speed was his speed; its strength was his strength. Despite the blood slicking his grip, Ben bared his teeth in a fierce smile. If Reive was still having to work against his dragon, fighting to keep the animal under control, Ben had the advantage now.

This time Reive was the one to make the first move. Ben's fierce grin widened as he recognized a variant of the same move he'd used moments ago. Reive learned fast, but he was still comparatively inexperienced, too much so to realize that Ben would recognize the move and know how to counter it. So when Reive feinted, Ben was there to meet him, not attacking but swiping his foot under Reive's and sending the humanform dragon tumbling to the ground.

Ben and his panther lunged to follow up the advantage, crashing onto Reive's chest to keep him down. Ben struck Reive's knife hand with the butt of his own knife, and as the knife fell from Reive's numb fingers, Ben pinned Reive's other arm and reversed his own knife.

It all happened in seconds and then he had the knife at Reive's throat, the shocked dark eyes looking up into his own.

He'd won their duel. All he had to do was thrust downward and the fight would be finished.

And he ... couldn't.

As he'd told Reive, he had his own brand of honor. He was, at heart, a cop, not a vigilante; he believed in justice and the rule of law. It simply wasn't in him to kill a helpless opponent. Especially an honorable opponent who was simply following orders and didn't want to be there any more than Ben did.

But even as these thoughts went through his mind, Reive's eyes flashed green and Ben realized he'd waited too long. Threatened, backed into a corner, faced with death,

Reive's self-preservation instinct had overcome his human mind.

He'd lost his grip on his dragon.

∾

Tessa stared at Heikon's face on the computer monitor. Beside her, Melody was still and silent with shock. Slowly, she slipped the chain back over her head. The crystal settled against her skin, feeling warm to the touch.

"What do you mean, *I'm* the Heart of the Hoard?" she asked. "How is that possible?"

"It was more common in the old days," Heikon said. "Few do it anymore. But it used to be common for that honor to be given to a living being—an animal or even a human. Not an object, but a friend. And your family have passed it down from generation to generation for what you would consider a long time. It's even been a long time for me, since I first made the arrangement with your great-grandsomething ... I don't know how many generations back, five or six at least. I was but a young dragon then. Your mother's family have served mine since then, even occasionally intermarrying with peripheral branches of the clan line."

"Wait, are you saying I have dragon blood in me?" No wonder Reive bore a slight resemblance to the face she saw every day in the mirror. They actually *were* relatives, albeit distant ones.

"Not enough to shift. But there is a kinship, yes." Heikon's face darkened, and Tessa was briefly glad that he was hundreds of miles away, not in the same room with her. "How have your parents neglected your education, telling you nothing of this? But what am I saying, what else should I expect of a pair of faithless traitors."

"Don't you dare talk about my parents that way," Tessa said coldly. "They haven't told me anything because they didn't get a chance. They're dead."

Heikon frowned. "Dead? So Reive has already accomplished his task. He didn't report it back to me. I'll have a word—"

"No, no." Tessa shook her head. "My parents died twenty years ago, when I was a small child. It's *me* that Reive is trying to kill."

"Then where did you get that stone you wear? From them?"

"I got it in a box of my parents' things, about two weeks ago."

"And that was when I became aware of the Heart again. Of course," Heikon murmured. "Tell me, child. What was the date of their death?"

Tessa steeled herself and told him.

"And where did they die? How?"

"Their car went off the road in the mountains in Colorado." She told him the location.

Heikon gazed at her, his face calm and thoughtful. He was like Darius in that way: she couldn't tell what he was thinking. Melody was like that a little bit, too. Maybe all dragons were.

"Which way were they driving?" he asked, finally.

"What do you mean?"

"Were they driving higher into the mountains, or driving back down?"

Tessa opened her mouth to say that she didn't know, but suddenly she *did* know. "They had just left me with a neighbor. It was night and I was sleepy. They told me they'd be back soon and put me down for a nap, and—" Her breath caught on a sob. She didn't have to finish. *And they never came back.*

"So they were driving *to* my lair," Heikon murmured. "They died on the road to my lair, not fleeing for the valley and leaving the mountains behind."

"Yes," Tessa said, wiping at her eyes. "The road where they died didn't go much of anywhere. Just deeper into the mountains." To a place like the one where Darius lived, she thought. Dragons must like high, lonely places.

"And first they put the Heartstone ... where? You received it recently, so it wasn't with them when they died. Or was it?"

"No," Tessa said. "It was in a safe deposit box along with some of their other things. I never even knew about it until their lawyer sent it to me. They'd left instructions that I wasn't to have it until I turned 21 ..."

She trailed off because the implications had never really struck her before. It was Melody who gave voice to the thought.

"They knew," Melody said softly. "Or, I suppose they couldn't have known for certain, but they must have suspected they might die."

"But *you* didn't know," Tessa said to Heikon. "They were coming to *warn* you."

"I had no idea. I believed that they fled with the Heartstone, and found some way to sever it from me, weakening me. Instead, all they did was put it away. I wouldn't have been able to sense it if it wasn't with its keepers. And I did, most assuredly, feel its loss. It was how my brother was able to defeat me, driving me wounded into exile and taking my place." Heikon's hands curled into fists on his desk.

"I don't understand," Tessa said. "If *I'm* the Heart—if my parents were—why does the stone matter at all?"

"Because it's their connection to me, child. Your connection to me. Had my brother been able to possess the stone, and your mother along with it, he could have destroyed both of them. He might as well have murdered me. Instead—"

163

He stopped.

"Instead he killed my mother," Tessa whispered. New tears welled in her eyes. "And my father along with her. He thought she had the stone with her. He killed her, killed them, because he was trying to kill *you*."

Heikon smiled grimly. "And very shocked he must have been, when he and his fellow conspirators burst into my lair and found me not crawling on the floor in agony, but ready for a fight, weakened slightly but still fierce. No wonder they were unable to kill me. As long as the Heartstone existed somewhere, I would still be as difficult to kill as dragon lords always are."

"But you ordered Reive to kill *me*; wouldn't that be the same as—"

"Not as long as the Heartstone is undamaged," Heikon said sharply. "I ordered Reive to execute your mother and bring me the stone, so I could find another, less faithless keeper to pass it along to."

"My mother *was* faithful!" Tessa flared. "And Reive is out there, right now, trying to kill my boyfriend, because *you* thought she wasn't!"

"Yes," Heikon murmured. "We really should do something about that."

"Yes, *thank* you! Can you talk to Reive, tell him—"

"*You* will," Heikon said. "Touch the Heartstone, child."

Tessa closed her hand over the stone resting above her heart. It seemed to her that it was so warm she could feel its heat through the decorative lace of her glove.

"Now that we are able to finally speak in person," Heikon said, "the connection may be forged in full, so that I can use you as my mouth and eyes."

Tessa's eyes went very wide. "I don't think I want—"

"Be silent. After this, you need not continue to be the Heart of the Hoard if you do not so choose. We can find someone else to take the stone. But for now, your mate needs you to be not a human girl-child, but the living Heart of the Hoard. Are you willing?"

Put like that, it was no choice at all. "Yes," Tessa said firmly. "If it'll help Ben—and please, he can't hold out forever. Please hurry."

"Close your eyes and focus on the stone," Heikon said, "and I will tell you what to do."

∼

Reive's dragon erupted from his human body, flinging Ben to the ground. The knife flew from his blood-slick hand and tumbled into the grass. It didn't matter; if bullets had little effect on a full-grown dragon, it wasn't as if a knife was going to do anything.

Reive lunged as he shifted, enormous jaws agape, jagged teeth flashing. Ben managed to turn his fall into a roll, tumbling out of the way a split second before he was crushed in those massive jaws. Reive snapped at dirt and grass instead.

Now? Ben's cat snarled, clawing to escape.

Now, he sighed, and let it come. Neither the human nor the panther had much of a chance, but he could last longer and run faster as a panther.

The borrowed tuxedo ripped off him, and Ben's panther landed four-footed on the grass, only to be met with a swipe from Reive's forepaw. Ben was knocked across the lawn, tumbling bruisingly into some ornamental bushes.

The dragon pursued him, pouncing like a cat. Reive's fighting style was very different now than it had been at the cabin, when he had been clearly in control, thinking and planning each move. This was pure hunting instinct. There was no human mind in charge here, just the hunting urges of a predatory animal.

Ben couldn't think how to snap him out of it. The only advantage he had now was his smaller size, enabling him to go places the dragon couldn't, and he took full advantage of it. Like a black streak he shot from the shrubbery toward the dark woods. Among the trees he might be able to get the drop on the dragon, or at least force Reive to hunt him until the human, rational mind regained control over the animal hindbrain.

There was a tremendous downdraft as Reive beat his wings and took to the air. Ben realized an instant later that the dragon wasn't flying, merely using his wings for a tremendous, assisted leap. Reive crashed to the ground between Ben and the woods, tearing great chunks out of the lawn. He lowered his head and hissed as Ben skidding to a stop.

Tail lashing, Ben crouched and then feinted right before jinking left. It was the exact same thing he'd done earlier (and that Reive had then tried on him) but he guessed correctly that Reive was too animalistic at the moment to recognize it. Reive snapped at empty air, and Ben shot past him, headed for the woods.

He almost made it. Almost. But the dragon was too huge and too fast. An enormous wing blocked Ben's path, and as he tried to veer around it, Reive caught Ben's panther in his great jaws.

It was almost over then and there, but Ben twisted wildly; he felt his fur and skin rake on the dragon's teeth and then he fell to the ground, bleeding—just in time for a slap of the dragon's forepaw to flatten him. He was pinned, as surely as ever a cat had pinned a mouse, and as Reive's jaws opened, the only thing Ben could think of was Tessa, her hands and her eyes and her brave, fighting spirit—

"Stop!"

The clear voice rang out through the night, and Ben, through blurred vision, saw a figure throw itself between him and the dragon's bloody jaws. For a dazed instant he thought he'd conjured up a hallucination of Tessa, but no, she was really there, standing defiantly over him. So small, so human—so fragile—

No! The cry rang out through his soul from the human inside him. He struggled to get up, fighting against the prison of Reive's claws. She was going to be killed.

Tiny and fragile and brave, she stood right between the dragon's front legs as Reive reared over her, jaws opening—

"Stop," Tessa said again, and this time it was not just her voice that spoke. There was something else under it, something deep and fierce and *old*.

Reive stopped.

For a long moment they remained like that, the dragon looking down at the woman, Ben sprawled on the ground with a great forepaw pinning him down. Then Reive rumbled, as sense began to come back into his eyes: "Heikon?"

"Stand *down*, boy," Tessa declared in that voice which had elements of her voice, but wasn't.

"This woman comes between me and my prey," Reive growled. "This woman *is* my prey."

"Not anymore," Tessa-Heikon commanded. "Stand down, Reive. Shift back and put your dragon away. Darius, are you there?"

"I am here," said the voice of Ben's father, not his human voice but the deep rumble of his dragon.

Ben turned his head, startled. He hadn't realized his father had shifted.

Darius's dragon was gunmetal gray, a darker version of Melody's silver, and so huge that even Reive's dragon looked comparatively small next to him. He was a clan leader at the height of his power, and the ground trembled slightly underfoot with each step he took as he came to stand beside Tessa. The tiny human woman barely came up to his shoulder.

Ben wondered dazedly how long his father had been watching the fight in dragon form, prepared to intervene if necessary. And how long *would* he have watched before stepping in?

Darius reached out one of his massive clawed forepaws to close over Reive's scaled wrist, above the claws holding Ben to the ground. The other dragon bowed his head and submitted, and Ben could suddenly breathe more easily as Reive's foot was lifted away in his father's firm grip.

"The hunt is over, child," Heikon said in Tessa's voice. "Honor is satisfied. You have done well. The conspirators are all gone now, and this woman is the loyal Heart of the—*Oh come on*, Heikon, you can talk to Reive on the computer right in the house there; do you really have to blather on about honor when no one is even helping my boyfriend who's bleeding to death?"

It was fascinating, Ben thought dizzily. He could hear the instant when her voice switched, the deep timbre of Heikon's rumble vanishing to leave only Tessa's familiar tones behind. And then she was kneeling beside him, gathering him into her lap, blood and dirt and all.

"Darius!" Tessa shouted. Ben's head was tipped back so all he could see was the night sky, no longer blocked by Reive's massive head. Had the dragon shifted back or simply moved? Ben couldn't tell, and it no longer seemed important anyway, because the threat was gone and his mate was holding him, and that was all that really mattered.

"Oh, *Ben!*" Melody's voice cried from not too far away, and Ben's last dazed thought was, *I guess the gang's all here ...*

And then, darkness.

CHAPTER 15

He was comfortable. Comfortable and warm. And ... human-shaped, not that it seemed to matter all that much. Nothing hurt. He was aware of his mate somewhere nearby.

Something was purring on his chest.

Ben cracked his eyes open. The small orange cat that Tessa called Toblerone was curled up on top of him, vibrating with a rumbling purr that seemed too large for its tiny size.

"I kept trying to move them off because I was afraid they'd hurt you," Tessa's voice said softly from somewhere nearby. "And they kept coming back. You didn't seem to mind having them there."

"They?" Ben murmured. He raised his head with some effort, but still no pain, though he could feel half-healed injuries tugging at his skin under the covers.

He was surrounded by cats. He didn't feel like counting, but most if not all of the kitten-herd was curled up around him, snuggled against his sides. Tessa had one of them in her lap. She was sitting beside his bed, and when he raised his gaze to her face, she smiled blindingly.

"Hi," she said, and leaned forward to cup his chin in hers, kissing him deeply.

The kitten in her lap made a protesting noise and jumped onto the bed.

"Mmmm," Tessa hummed into his mouth. She pulled back and kept caressing the side of his face as she asked, "How do you feel? Do you need anything?"

His sleep-logged brain mulled that over for a moment. "Water? You don't have to; I can get it—" He started trying to sit up, but as Toblerone sank his claws into the blanket, Tessa pushed them both back down.

"Just stay there. I'll get it."

She was back in a moment with a glass of water. The fog was clearing from Ben's head, enough to notice that he was in the big four-poster bed in the Lilac Room, which at least answered his question about whether they were still at Darius's. He relocated Toblerone to the side of the bed and managed to push himself up on the pillows enough that Tessa didn't have to hold the glass for him like a total invalid.

Further inspection determined that he was naked. Now that he was sitting up, Ben pushed down the blanket to his waist so he could examine the purple, healing claw marks and a neat row of half-healed puncture wounds down his side, left by Reive's teeth.

"Your father said it would heal better if it wasn't bandaged. I remember you saying something like that too, back at the motel." Tessa twisted her hands together. "Does it hurt?"

"Not really. It's just itchy. I'm going to be starving when I wake up a little more, but right now I just want to sit here for a while." He rested his head against the pillows and rolled it to the side to take a better look at her. She was wearing a loose dark-green sweater that looked like one of Melody's. With its high turtleneck, he couldn't tell if she had the necklace on. All that really mattered was ... "You look beautiful."

Tessa blew out a breath. "Flattery will get you everywhere." She leaned in to kiss him again.

"You were amazing out there," Ben told her when she drew away.

"Do you remember it? You were pretty out of it for awhile there." A tense undercurrent to her voice lingered, a remnant of past worry.

"I remember you standing up to Reive. Incredible." He frowned. "*I'm* the one who's supposed to protect *you.*"

"You did. I'd never have had the time to call Heikon if you hadn't held him off. Not to mention saving me about a million other times in the past few days. Anyway, we're a partnership." She closed her lips on his, and murmured against his mouth, "We protect each other."

Ben smiled against her lips.

"Well, this is cozy," a deep voice said, and they jerked apart as Darius strode into the room. Close on his heels came someone else, a tall, lean man with iron-gray hair and a dignified bearing that reminded Ben uncomfortably of his father.

Tessa scrambled to her feet, and Ben pulled up the blanket to cover his bare chest. "Have any of you people ever heard of knocking?" he asked irritably.

"I heard talking in here, so I knew you were awake," Darius said, dismissing the issue with a peremptory motion of his hand. "Anyway, Heikon has to fly this evening, and he wanted to talk to both of you for a minute."

"Oh ... you're Heikon." Ben took another look at the gray-haired stranger. There was a resemblance to Reive, come to think of it: the same bronze skin and deep-set dark eyes.

Heikon dipped his head in acknowledgement. "And you're

Benedict Keegan. I owe you and your mate a great honor-debt."

"A what now?" Tessa said.

"Because of my misjudgment, you both nearly died. In addition to that, you've done me a great service by restoring my most valuable property." He smiled at Tessa. "Which I've come to reclaim."

"Oh." She reached down the collar of her sweater and pulled up the silver chain. For just an instant, she hesitated, and then pulled it over her head in a single quick motion, for the last time. With the necklace in hand, she hesitated again.

"It's not too late to change your mind," Heikon said. "It's yours by right and tradition. And your actions as my voice indicated to me that you are well worthy of being the brightest jewel in my collection."

It was the last sentence that seemed to change her mind. Tessa shook her head. "I'm a jewel in no one's collection. Except maybe Ben's." She gave Ben a brilliant smile that took his breath away, and held out the necklace. Heikon gravely accepted it in his palm. He tucked it into a pocket of his gray overcoat.

"So now what?" Tessa asked, following the necklace with her eyes until it could no longer be seen. "I don't feel any different."

"You won't, though you may yearn for the necklace from time to time. But I will find a new Heart for my hoard, and soon you won't think of it."

"I'll always think of it, I expect," she murmured, touching her chest where the crystal used to rest.

Darius had been standing patiently to one side, watching the proceedings with interest; now he said, "And you have a promise for my son, do you not?"

"For both your son and his mate," Heikon said. "As I said

earlier, I owe you an honor-debt. I will have a gift for your firstborn, when he or she is old enough."

"Not the Heart of the Hoard, I hope," Tessa said quickly.

Heikon smiled. "No, no. Not that." He lifted a hand in a wordless farewell and turned to go.

"Wait," Ben called after him. "She's not pregnant *yet*, is she? Tessa, you're not—"

"Not that I know of." She kissed him on the forehead. "Calm down."

"First panthers, now half-human grandchildren," Darius sighed. One of the kittens rubbed on his leg and he looked down with an exasperated expression. "And all these damned *cats*." But he leaned down to pick it up, supporting its hindquarters as Tessa had shown him. The kitten began to purr.

"Oh, you can't fool me," Tessa said, looking over at him with her hand on Ben's shoulder. "You're going to be one of those grandfathers who spoils his grandchildren shamelessly."

"I sincerely hope that grandcats are the only thing I'll have to deal with for the near future," Darius said. "The two of you are trouble enough. And you're going to need calories for all that healing. I'll have a meal sent up, with plenty of red meat."

"Speaking of which," Tessa said, "I believe you promised me the recipe for your very excellent soup, didn't you? We all got kind of busy with the whole assassin thing."

Darius raised an eyebrow. "You were serious about that."

"Dead serious."

The corner of his mouth quirked. "I'll speak to the kitchen about it. You'll have it before the day is out."

He left ... taking the kitten with him.

After a pause, Ben said, "You and my father are certainly getting along well. I'm not sure whether to be pleased or disturbed."

"I think it's easier for me, without the weight of all the history between you," Tessa said. "Also, in spite of all his arrogance, I think he really doesn't mind having someone stand up to him. Some people just want someone to argue with."

"I've *tried* arguing with him. It doesn't help."

"Not like that. Like ... Oh, I don't know how to explain it. He doesn't intimidate me; I've dealt with worse. And I think he likes that."

Ben looked up at her. "You've dealt with worse than *my father*? He's a dragon. Also a mobster, I don't know if I mentioned that part."

"Your sister did already. But listen, you should try dealing with a mom who's just been told that little Bobby can't have one of our cats because dear little Bobby just spent the last ten minutes terrorizing the feral cat room and had to be escorted out with a hand on his collar."

"Okay, you've got a point." He reached up to touch the smooth, soft curve of her neck behind her ear. "So what was all that with the necklace and Heikon? The Heart of the Hoard, I guess it's called."

"The Heart of the Hoard is ... more complicated than that. I'll tell you all about it, but maybe not just now." She turned her head, gazing in the direction Heikon had gone, with a wistful look on her face.

Ben pulled her hand to his lips and kissed her fingers. "Do you miss it?"

"No, not really. Well, yes, but only because it was my parents'. They were innocent, you know. Heikon thought they betrayed him, but they were loyal all along."

"They were good people," Ben said quietly.

"Yes," she murmured. He could see the gleam of unshed tears in her eyes, and reached up to pull her down so that her soft head rested in the crook of his shoulder, her body half on and half off the bed.

"I owe you an apology," Ben said.

"What?" Tessa started to raise her head. "Whatever for?"

Ben pushed her head gently back into the crook of his neck. "For earlier. I could see you felt out of place here. I do too. I don't know why I didn't say anything; I guess ..." He heaved a sigh. "I've spent so long play-acting for my dad, pretending that I fit in here ... I suppose I do it automatically now. But I shouldn't have let it come between us. You were feeling alienated, isolated, and I wasn't helping."

"It's so odd to me how easily you can read me," she murmured. "Most people can't."

In Ben's chest, his panther was purring. "I've always been pretty good at people. I'm just sorry that I didn't catch on right away to how you were feeling."

Tessa laced her fingers through his. "I could have said something. Maybe we both need some practice at this whole relationship thing."

"We'll figure it out," he said softly into her hair. "I love you, Tessa."

She made a little breath-catching noise, and then very quietly, so quietly he could barely hear her: "I love you, too." There was a silence, then she added, "I've never said that to anyone before. At least not that I remember."

Ben's heart shattered into a tiny little pieces. God, the life she'd lived. He had often been frustrated with his family, he'd frequently had cause to doubt his father's affection for him, but he had still grown up with a mother who loved him. Thinking of Tessa being so alone ... it hurt more than being torn up by a dragon's jaws, more than a thousand slashes from draconian claws.

But at least this time, he knew better than to stay quiet and let her suffer in silence. *Never again.* "You can say it to me as many times as you like," he said. "And I'll say it back to you. You're not alone now, Tessa. You'll never be alone again."

She sighed and turned her face into his neck, and for a little while he just held her like that. Finally she pushed herself up. "Is this uncomfortable? Am I hurting you?"

"No. In fact ..." He put his arms around her, pulling her all the way onto the bed. She toppled beside him with a delighted squeal. "I'll show you exactly how much better I'm feeling."

Which of course was the moment someone knocked on the door.

"That's probably the food my dad was having sent up." Ben kissed her. "We could make them go away."

"No. You need it to heal. Anyway ..." She kissed him again, long and lingering. "We're going to want to save something for dessert."

CHAPTER 16

Tessa set the last box down and looked around the inside of the cabin.

Over the last few months, she had watched the cabin go from being a wreck (for the second time, from what Ben had told her) to getting spruced up to its previous rustic glory. She and Ben had come out on weekends, and she'd learned to cut and sand and finish wood. They'd also had unexpected help on a couple of those weekends. Reive had shown up, quiet and polite, with a pair of work gloves and a willingness to help. Tessa still wasn't entirely sure she trusted him. But he wanted to help fix what he'd destroyed, and she respected that.

Now the hills around Autumn Grove were flushed with brilliant colors, flaming red and gold in the mountain foothills, and soon she would spend her first winter outside the city since she was a small child.

"You still sure about this?" Ben asked quietly behind her.

"This is a fine time to ask me, now that I've quit my job and all." But she was smiling when she turned around and slid her arms around his waist.

She was going to miss the cat rescue, just like Ben was going to miss working for a big-city police department. But she was also excited and eager at the idea of living here. There were so many new possibilities for both of them. The local sheriff's department had offered Ben a position, and he and Derek had renewed their discussion about starting their own private security-consulting business. Tessa was a lot less sure what she wanted to do with herself. She thought that for a little, while she might just try some different things. Volunteer with different places in town. Look into taking some online courses. All she knew was, she wanted to do something to make a difference, like she had at the shelter. She just needed to find somewhere she felt like she fit.

It was a fresh start for both of them. A new life.

And she might not even have to start all over at making new friends. She'd shown Melody the bookstore space in downtown Autumn Grove, and she was pretty sure Melody was already in talks to lease it. Of course, it was easier to do that kind of thing when your dad was loaded. But Melody had dreamed of owning her own bookstore for a long time. And even if they wouldn't be working right across the street from each other, they'd still be neighbors.

Yeah. She was looking forward to finding out what living in the country was like. And if she didn't enjoy it, well, they could try something else.

Their future was wide open.

"Mrrrowww!"

... okay, one thing about the future she'd already determined was that it was going to have a lot of cats in it.

After the cats' long ride from the city in their new, large, hard-sided carrier, she'd put them in the bedroom with food, water, and a litter tray, just like the first time she'd brought them here, but a little better prepared this time around. It hadn't taken them long, this time, to start wander out into the cabin. They weren't really kittens anymore, more like teenage cats now, gangly and growing into their fully adult size. But they were still very curious and eager to look around. They'd already been up to the cabin a few more times, accompanying Tessa and Ben on their weekend excursions, so it wasn't totally new.

This would be a better place for them than Ben's apartment, she thought. There had never been enough space for them there, even if there weren't quite as many cats as there used to be. But these cats would really enjoy their new home. The cabin was full of railings to climb on and corners to creep into. She and Ben had kept most of them, but Toblerone, the bold little orange one, was now a permanent resident of Darius's mansion. Tessa had worried that he'd be lonely without his brothers and sisters, but the last time she'd seen him, he was being petted and pampered by Darius's entire staff, and had a shiny new collar studded with what she sincerely hoped were rhinestones but had a bad feeling might be actual diamonds. Even if Darius was too busy for him most of the time, she had a feeling he was going to be the world's most well-petted cat. He and Maddox seemed to nurse a cordial loathing for each other, though.

"Penny for your thoughts," Ben murmured, brushing her cheek with the back of his hand.

She smiled involuntarily. "It's probably not anything you're expecting. I was actually wondering about that bodyguard of your dad's, if that's the right word—"

"I prefer 'henchman', but go on."

"Yeah ... I was wondering what he turns into, if you ever found out."

"No idea." Ben smiled. "You could just ask my dad, since apparently you two are besties now."

"*Besties*? As if."

179

"So you claim, but I don't even remember the last time he called me, and now he emails you all the time."

"No he doesn't."

"Tessa, he just sent you an email the other day asking if you'd had a chance to use that recipe yet, and reminding you that—"

"—'revenge is a dish best served cold,' I know, so I need to be sure and cool it down properly before serving it. Yes, I remember." She stroked her fingers through Ben's dark hair. "It's not that I've forgiven him for all those years he treated you so poorly. It's just easier if—"

"Tessa, trust me, I don't care if you hang around with my dad. Honestly, if you want to do all the interacting with my dad for the entire household, *please*, go right ahead. I'll be completely happy to never talk to him again."

She leaned up to kiss him. "He does care about you, you know. And he's proud of you, I think. In his own way."

"You know what?" Ben said, and he swept her off her feet into a bridal carry. Tessa let out a startled shriek and clutched at him. "Let's stop talking about my dad. There are a lot of things I'd much rather think about."

"Like?" she asked, winding her arms around his neck.

"Like a bed upstairs that's freshly made and needs to be properly christened." He nuzzled against her hair.

Tessa grinned and wriggled a little closer, pressing against his chiseled chest. It didn't seem to matter how many times she had this man; she still wanted more. "I think that sounds like a fantastic way to welcome each other home."

∽

They were lying upstairs in sated bliss, twined together and drowsing, when Ben suddenly raised his head. "Do you hear an engine?"

She didn't at first, but in the perfect stillness of the afternoon, it came to her eventually: the rising and falling of a car or truck laboring up the winding driveway. A moment later, the engine noise became clear as it drove out of the woods into the clearing around the cabin.

Ben rose quietly and went to the window, then turned back to her with a grin. "It's Derek and Gaby. Looks like they brought the family."

As they went down the stairs—Ben buttoning his shirt and Tessa trying to smooth down the disarray of her short hair—there was a knock at the door that sent the cats running for cover.

"Hey there," Derek said, grinning at them as Ben opened the door. "We decided to be good neighbors and bring you a pie. Where do you want it?"

"Ooh, what kind of pie?" Tessa asked, craning around him. "Hi, Gaby."

"Hi," Derek's mate said with a smile. She was carrying their new baby in a front-mounted sling and holding their son Sandy by the hand.

Tessa had met their family a few times; she and Ben had gone into Gaby's café in downtown Autumn Grove more than once (and would become regulars now that they lived here, Tessa knew; the food was as good as promised) and they had also visited Derek and Gaby in their old farmhouse just outside town. But this was Tessa's first time having them in *her* house.

Mine. Ben's. Ours.

She went to start a pot of coffee, then showed Sandy how to properly hold and pet the cats, who had crept out of hiding to investigate the new arrivals. Tessa was cautious at first, having dealt with cats in the shelter who had been hurt by overly enthusiastic children, but Sandy was a good student, paying close attention and carefully copying the things she taught him. Tessa got out some of the cat toys, and left Sandy and the kittens happily playing while the adults took their coffee out onto the porch.

"So you guys are moving up here for good," Derek said. "You're really doing it."

Tessa nodded. "We've already given up the lease on my place. I wasn't attached to it anyway." She had moved in with Ben almost as soon as they'd gotten back from Darius's mansion.

"And we're keeping mine through the end of the year," Ben said, "just in case something comes up or we change our minds."

"But I don't expect we will." Tessa looked around at the wind-ruffled meadow and the red-and-gold brilliance of the forest, decked out in its autumn finery.. "It's amazing here. I think the first time I came here, I knew I'd come home; I just didn't let myself admit it yet."

Ben smiled. "Wait until you go through a winter out here before you say that for sure. This place sometimes gets snowed in for days at a time."

Gaby laughed. Tessa had taken an instant liking to her; the friendly café owner had shown her nothing but kindness, welcoming Ben's new mate into her family's life. "Snowed in for days, with nothing to do except entertain yourselves in the cabin? How very difficult for you. I'm sure you won't be able to find *anything* to do." She winked at Derek.

Ben was actually blushing. Tessa reached out and took his hand. "I think you're right," she said. "We'll figure something out."

Which was, in some sense, the story of their entire relationship. She never would have dreamed when Ben had walked through the door of the cat rescue, when she'd gotten so mad at Melody for interfering in her life, that she would be sitting here, on the porch of a place so peaceful and quiet where she felt perfectly at ease, starting to find her way into a new family and a new life.

I finally have a place to belong.

∾

If you'd like to read more about Ben, Tessa, Melody, Darius, Derek, and Gaby, keep reading with
Bear in a Bookshop!

He's all wrong for her, so why do his arms feel so right? Tattooed ex-con Gunnar and shy bookworm Melody must find a way to write their own happy ending before their pasts catch up with them and ruin their chance at happiness forever.

Now available on Amazon and Kindle Unlimited!

A NOTE FROM ZOE CHANT

Thank you for buying my book! I hope you enjoyed it. If you'd like to be emailed when I release my next book, please click here to be added to my mailing list: http://www.zoechant.com/join-my-mailing-list/. You can also visit my webpage at zoechant.com or follow me on Facebook or Twitter. You are also invited to join my VIP Readers Group on Facebook!

Please consider reviewing *Pet Rescue Panther*, even if you only write a line or two. I appreciate all reviews, whether positive or negative.

Cover art: © Depositphoto.com

If you enjoyed this book, you might also like my paranormal
romance and sci-fi romance written as Lauren Esker!

CPSIA information can be obtained
at www.ICGtesting.com
Printed in the USA
LVHW032239050921
697067LV00015B/192